the adventures of

hashbrown
winters

To Riley,
Keep Reading the Oracle!

the adventures of

hashbRown
winters

Frank L. Cole

Bonneville Books
Springville, Utah

ISBN 13: 978-1-59955-303-0

Published by Bonneville Books, an imprint of Cedar Fort, Inc., 2373 W. 700 S., Springville,
UT 84663
Distributed by Cedar Fort, Inc., www.cedarfort.com

LIBRARY OF CONGRESS CATALOGING-IN-PUBLICATION DATA

Cole, Frank L., 1977–
The Adventures of Hashbrown Winters / Frank L. Cole.
p. cm.
Summary: When he accidentally injures the school bully's pet cockroach,
eleven-year-old Hashbrown and his friends come up with a plan to thwart the
hooligan's designs for revenge.
ISBN 978-1-59955-303-0
[1. Bullies--Fiction. 2. Friendship--Fiction. 3. Schools--Fiction.] I.
Title.
PZ7.C673435Ad 2009
[Fic]--dc22

2009009332

Illustrations by Adam Record
Cover design by Jen Boss
Cover design © 2009 by Lyle Mortimer
Edited and typeset by Heidi Doxey

Printed in Canada
10 9 8 7 6 5 4 3 2 1

Printed on acid-free paper

For Heidi, who always laughs
even when I'm not funny.

Praise for Frank L. Cole and
The Adventures of Hashbrown Winters

Frank is a wizard; he's a fantastic story teller who can turn the ordinary into gold and make me thrilled to read about every second of it. This is a great book. Sure it's got page numbers and chapters, and those things are cool, but most importantly, it has one great story—read it.

> Obert Skye,
> author of *Leven Thumps and the Gateway to Foo*

The moment Flinton "Hashbrown" Winters smashes a dog-sized, talking cockroach with his lucky marble, you know this will not be a typical adventure. Hashbrown, Snow Cone, Four Hips, Whiz, and the rest of his friends will have you laughing out loud. Frank L. Cole has created a wonderfully funny story with enough twists and turns to keep children and adults glued to their seats.

> J. Scott Savage,
> author of *Farworld: Water Keep*

An excellent book. You'll be laughing a lot as you sit on the edge of your seat. Highly recommended.

> James Dashner,
> author of *The 13th Reality: The Hunt for Dark Infinity*

Acknowledgments

I have many people to thank for helping this book become a reality. My parents for feeding me stories at breakfast, lunch, and dinner. My brother Michael, the funniest guy in the world and the only person I know who believes there are hyenas roaming wild in Kansas. To Jennifer, for bleeding on every one of my pages and never pulling a punch. To Ethan for being my guinea pig. To Kevin, the Oracle—how did you ever fit in locker 366? To Jeff, my very own Fibber Mckenzie.

Of course I'd be nowhere without my publisher, Cedar Fort; my editor, Heidi Doxey; and my illustrator, Adam Record, who helped Hashbrown really come to life. Thanks guys for laughing at my work.

I have to thank my children, Jackson, Gavin, and Camberlyn, aka Hashbrown, Snow Cone, and Misty Piccolo.

And lastly, I thank my wife, Heidi, who I struggled to listen to while she pulled so much of my stuff out of the garbage and would never let me quit. You can toss the Q-tips now, Heidi, I'm pretty sure they've been used. Gross!

Contents

1. Piñata's Secret Weapon   1
2. Puddle of Goop   8
3. We're Not Talking Ketchup   16
4. The Wonderful Misty Piccolo   29
5. Thus Sayeth the Oracle   34
6. Hambone's Discovery   41
7. Jimmy Cracked Corn   47
8. Purple Duck Floaters   53
9. Sandwiched   58
10. Whiz's Tale   71
11. Showdown by the Oak Tree   78
12. Heartbroken   89

Wisdom of the Oracle   95
Discussion Questions   99
About the Author   100

Chapter 1

Piñata's Secret Weapon

Every night just before bed, my mother always told me, "Hashbrown, one day you'll do great things." As I sat there, hiding next to a large, reeking dumpster with my best friend Snow Cone on one side and my pal Measles on the other, I couldn't help but wonder just what she meant by that.

"I think they spotted us, Hashbrown," Snow Cone said as several red paintballs exploded on the ground next to our hideout. "Perhaps hiding behind the dumpster was a poor choice."

"Don't I know it," I said. "We're standing out like one of Lips Warshowski's cold sores. How could I be so stupid?"

Measles grabbed my collar, pressing his red splotched face practically in my ear. "They're using red paint. Red paint, Hashbrown! I'm allergic to red paint. I'm going to break out in hives!"

"I thought you were allergic to all paint," Snow Cone said.

Measles blinked. "That's right, I am! Oh boy, this is not good. Why are we playing paintball again?"

"Because we always play paintball on Saturdays, Measles," I said, scratching my head in frustration.

"Yeah, but not on my birthday," Measles moaned.

"Your birthday's in March," Snow Cone said.

"Oh yeah. What month is this?"

"October!" Snow Cone and I shouted in unison.

I guess you couldn't blame him. Memory loss is a common side effect for someone who's had measles on three separate occasions. Several more paintballs burst on the rocks next to the dumpster.

"These guys are terrible shots," I said.

Snow Cone craned his neck to get a better look and smiled. "What do you expect from Pot Roast and Stilts?"

"You're kidding me. That's who's shooting at us?"

Snow Cone nodded, a big grin stretching across his face.

Gregory "Pot Roast" Oberham and Ethan "Stilts" Drubbers were legally blind, and their helmets wouldn't allow them to wear glasses. They couldn't pass an eye exam if the letters were written on a billboard.

A warm breeze whipped around the dumpster, bringing with it a ray of hope for our small team. It also brought a very disgusting odor of rotting tuna fish.

Snow Cone pinched his nose. "Seriously, Hashbrown, why a dumpster?"

Some third grader appeared on the field looking very puzzled. He wore a scouting uniform and stared down cross-eyed at a compass. When he saw the three of us hiding behind the dumpster, his eyes lit up.

"Oh good, I found somebody," he said, adjusting his glasses. "Do you guys know where I can find Blimpy Park? I think I'm lost."

The boy was unarmed, and we were almost positive he wasn't on either one of our teams, but we weren't taking any chances.

We quickly fired our weapons at him, transforming his khaki shirt into a multi-colored mess in a matter of seconds.

"I hate day camp!" he screamed, chucking his compass to the side and running wildly back in the direction he came.

"Just another innocent casualty," Measles said, scratching his hip. More enemy fire peppered the ground.

"Look, if they're the only two left, I think we should take them," I said.

"I don't know, Hash," Snow Cone said. "Whiz nabbed Hopscotch by the rope bridge about two minutes ago. Roast and Stilts are the only ones I can see guarding the flag, but there could be more out there. It's too risky."

Suddenly the sound of heavy wheezing cut through the air. I flinched, expecting the worst, but was relieved to see Four Hips Dixon crawling toward me, his enormous belly pouring out from beneath his camouflaged T-shirt.

"Four Hips is here," I said, grabbing Four Hips by his sleeve and dragging him up beside us.

"Yeah, I know. I saw him coming for a while," Snow Cone answered. "I just assumed the battle would be over by the time he arrived."

"Hey, that's not funny," Four Hips said, coughing into his hands. "I've never ran so much in my life."

"What are you talking about?" Snow Cone squawked. "You crawled the entire time."

"So?"

I looked over at my portly friend. "Ah, Four Hips, you're already out!" I hissed, glancing down at his shirt.

"Huh?" He looked up at me in confusion.

"You've been hit like three times." I pointed to several obvious stains tagged around his mid-section.

"What?" Four Hips shouted in panic and examined his

shirt. He wiped sweat from his forehead and gave a sigh of relief. "No, that's just jelly. You had me going there for a second."

"Jelly? Where did you get jelly?" Measles asked.

"I brought my own jar, duh. Do you want some?"

Measles shook his head. It figured Four Hips had found a way to bring along the most unusual snacks for our battle.

"Look, I say we make our move." I crouched and checked my hopper for paintballs.

"Hashbrown wait for reinforcements!" Snow Cone ordered. "Don't you remember what Piñata Gonzales said? They have a secret weapon on their team. Besides, Whiz should be here any second now. Where is he?"

"Piñata was bluffing as usual. If they had a secret weapon, we would have seen it by now," I argued. "It's now or never." Readying my weapon, I plucked a small glass orb from my pocket and gave it a kiss. It was a marble, but not just any old marble. It was my bull basher; my most prized possession. It brought me luck.

"I say we wait for Whiz," Four Hips wheezed. "I don't feel like crawling anymore, and I think my can of Easy Cheese just exploded in my pocket."

Refusing to listen to the advice of my friends, I sprung up from behind the dumpster with paintball gun blazing. Pot Roast was the first to drop when Stilts, shocked to see me running at them, accidentally pulled his trigger splattering red paint across Pot Roast's chest. He belched out an agonizing groan. "I'm done for!" he shouted. "Tell my ma I went down fighting!"

Stilts spun around, finger squeezing the trigger, sending a spray of red balls whizzing through the air like kamikaze hornets. I was quick on my feet and barrel rolled just as the bullets cut above my helmet. With lightning speed I aimed

at Stilts and sprayed him with thirty rounds of my own peri-
winkle blue paintballs.

"Brilliant. Absolutely brilliant," Snow Cone shouted
from behind the dumpster. I couldn't help but grin. Clearly
my moves had impressed Snow. I gave him a triumphant
thumb's up, tapping my trusty paintball gun against my
chest. "Retreat!" Snow Cone screamed.

I smiled but shook my head. "Say again, good buddy?"
I dug my finger in my ear. Retreat? What was he talking
about? Shouldn't he be screaming something like "victory,"
or "three cheers for Hashbrown," or. . . ?

"Retreat, Hashbrown!" Four Hips appeared from behind
the cover of the dumpster, hopping up and down like a possessed orca. Four Hips, Snow Cone, and Measles flung their
paintball guns into the air and charged off in the other direction. Out of the corner of my visor, a giant figure blazed
into view. It was a setup. Pot Roast and Stilts were only
decoys, and now Hambone Oxcart, Pordunce Elementary
School's number one bully, was barreling down upon me
toting a massive cardboard tube in his arms. He was the
secret weapon!

Hambone looked like a bearded brontosaurus, crashing
through the trees and trampling anything standing in his
way. Where did he come from? How did Piñata Gonzales
convince Hambone to play on his team? More importantly,
what in the world was he holding?

I tried to run, but it was useless. Hambone covered the
distance in merely a few lumbering strides. In a final attempt
to save myself, I fired my paintball gun directly at Hambone.
The bullets simply bounced off his muscular chest as if it
were bulletproof.

Grinning, he positioned the tube on his shoulder, revealing a can of fluorescent yellow paint emptying into the rear.

It was no ordinary cardboard tube. No, it was a paintball bazooka!

Ka-blam!

I blacked out for a solid minute. When I awoke, Piñata Gonzales and Staples Ardmore stood dangling our captured flag above my head like a kite. I looked like one of my younger sister's finger paintings.

"I told you to wait," Snow Cone said, slugging me in the shoulder as the two of us, heavily plastered with paint, exited the course and headed toward our bicycles. It was a heartbreaking loss. My team had gone undefeated two years in a row.

"I don't get it," I said, skimming paint from my chin with a squeegee. "Since when did Piñata become friends with Hambone? Hambone doesn't have any friends. He beats everyone up." It just didn't make sense. Hambone Oxcart ruled elementary school. No one messed with him. Not even the teachers.

Snow Cone grabbed my arm and pulled me behind a tree. "There's the reason," he whispered. Through the cover of branches we saw Piñata Gonzales, Petrol Giminski, and Staples Ardmore handing Hambone a stack of comic books and some green dollar bills. "They paid him off."

"Dirty little boogers," I said. "They stepped over the line."

"Yeah, but what are we going to do about it? We can't cross Hambone."

My blood boiled as we crept away from the trees. "Where was Whiz anyway?" I asked.

"Nature called," Whiz said, poking his head up from behind his bike. In his hand he clutched a plastic bag filled with a dampened pair of blue jeans. He now wore a pair of pink and green shorts, two sizes too small and decorated with tiny paintball helmets. "I got these for cheap at the gift shop," he said, staring down proudly at his new clothing.

"That's gross, Whiz," I said and took a step back to give him some room.

Chapter 2
Puddle of Goop

The following Monday morning, I stood at my locker while Snow Cone griped about our loss. "I'm serious, Hashbrown. If you're not going to listen to my instructions, I refuse to play anymore."

"I know, I know," I said, unzipping my backpack and pulling out my schoolbooks. Snow Cone was blaming our loss on me, which was fair to a point, but neither one of us had any idea Hambone would be the secret weapon.

Perhaps it's time for a proper introduction. My real name is Flinton Deanderbow Winters, but I have gone by Hashbrown since the first grade when I challenged Butter Bibowski to a hash brown eating contest and won. I ended up in the hospital for a week, but I earned my nickname. In fact, if you ask for me by any other name, I don't think I'd answer you.

At Pordunce Elementary School, if you don't have a nickname, you really don't exist. In fact, when I started grade school, I simply had to do something to get myself a name, or die trying. I just about did. After the throw down with Butter, I was haunted for months with a recurring nightmare of an army of grease-battered hash brown soldiers hosing me down with a shower of sticky cheese sauce. Sadly, every Wednesday I have to relive that nightmare when Ms. Borfish, the school's chef, strikes up the ovens and crisps those puppies to a golden brown.

Pierre Yosepa Jones, also known as Snow Cone, is my best friend. We would do anything for each other, but right now he was getting on my nerves. "Look, can we talk about something else?" I asked. I looked over my shoulder as I cycled through my locker combination. You could never know who might be spying in the hallways these days. With a sharp clang, my locker door popped open, revealing a poster of Velcro Splinter Man in a heated battle with his archenemy, Beluga Bart.

"Cool poster." It was Bubblegum Bulkins, slouching against the lockers and chomping on an entire package of raspberry flavored Cow Cud bubble gum.

"Bulkins, don't sneak up on us like that," I said, clutching my heart. "And where were you on Saturday?"

"Hey, I had an emergency, but, oh yeah, I heard about the disaster," Bulkins said, smirking. "You're a loose cannon, Hashbrown."

"What do you mean emergency?" Snow Cone asked.

Bubblegum frowned, staring down at the dirt beneath his fingernails. "I popped one of my bubbles next to Yogurt's ear, temporarily deafening him. We had to take him to the veterinarian." Yogurt was Bubblegum's hyperactive pet Chihuahua. "Besides, from what I heard, it wouldn't have mattered if I'd been there or not. What with Hashbrown runnin' and gunnin'." He flashed his fingers as if they were pistols and chuckled.

"Whatever," I said. The first period bell rattled above our heads, and I crammed my books into the locker.

"We'll see you in Ms. Pinken's class," Bulkins said as he

and Snow Cone trotted off toward their first class. To be honest, I hadn't stopped thinking about my paintball blunder since Saturday afternoon. I couldn't sleep, for crying out loud. Bubblegum needed to get his priorities straight. His little yapping dog would benefit from some hearing loss. If only he had been there, maybe we could've won. Ah, who am I kidding? It was my fault. I'm usually on my game, but for some reason I never saw that ambush coming.

Just then a giant shadow fell across my locker. I immediately recognized a strange odor. "Pay up," Hambone Oxcart's baritone voice rumbled from behind me. I swiveled, looking up at the towering man-child. His enormous chin was black with stubble.

"Hey Hambone, great game on Saturday. Where did you get that bazooka from?" I whimpered.

"My what?" Hambone asked, a baffled expression forming on his face.

"Uh . . . That big 'boom-boom' you shot me with?" I had to dumb it down for the big fella if I wanted him to understand.

"Oh, that . . . I don't remember. Now pay me my money."

I looked down at my watch and noted the date. It was October 15, but to Hambone it was payday. Hambone was your typical bully in the sense that he stole your lunch money, but unique because he set up a very generous payment plan. With the ever-growing student population, Hambone gave the students at Pordunce the option of paying two weeks' worth of lunch money on the first and the fifteenth of the month. It was actually pretty brilliant. Hambone's fingers curled into a fist, and I caught sight of yet another alarming image. Hambone's pet cockroach, Phil, scurried up out of his pocket and rested on his shoulder.

"Isn't today a holiday?" I asked.

Hambone scowled. "Yeah, for me."

I moaned. I was really hoping to spend that money on a new velvet carrying satchel for my marbles. I could see Hambone was growing impatient, so I quickly fished my wallet from my pants pocket and handed him a crumpled five dollar bill.

Hambone glared at the money and then back up at me. "Don't you read?"

"Why yes, thank you, I learned how in first grade. Didn't you?" I asked, hoping this was Hambone's way of making small talk.

"Ha, ha, very funny. My pa told me it said in the newspaper that oil prices are on the rise," he growled.

"Good to know," I said, trying to squeeze past his enormous body. Hambone grabbed me by my shirt sleeve and slammed me against the lockers.

"Not so fast. I don't know what my pa meant, but I'm gonna need another dollar from you," he said, gnawing on his hairy lip.

"Another dollar?" I yelled, but quickly caught myself. "Of course you do." I handed him another dollar. "And might I add that Phil looks more and more like . . . uh . . . you, every day." I was just trying to be polite, but my words obviously made Hambone angry. He roared, Phil hissed, and I just about soiled my jeans. Luckily, the late bell blared overhead. Hambone thundered off, leaving me penniless at my locker.

You're probably thinking I'm just a big coward, right? Why didn't I just stand up to him? Why didn't I just report him to the principal? Why didn't I send up the Bat Signal? Blah, blah, blah.

Let me explain something to you. Hambone Oxcart is no ordinary fifth grader. His mother's a rhinoceros, and his dad fell from space on the back of a meteor. I kid you not. Hambone's feet are enormous. They are so big he once stepped on both of Timothy Kiegan's feet at the same time and snapped every single one of his toes. It took both school nurses and Mr. Hemroin, the P.E. teacher, to turn his toes back in the right direction. We know him now as Toeless Kiegan, and to this day, he walks with a limp.

Do you want to know what's worse? Hambone's his real name. No one dares give him another. Oh sure, I've thought of dozens that fit him perfectly, like Sasquatch, or Ogre Turd, or . . . you get the point. Of course, Hambone is nowhere near when I talk about him.

I once heard from a trusted source, Fibber McKenzie, Hambone was spotted one night eating part of a fence behind the school playground. No one believed it at first, but the next day in third period math, Hambone walked in with splinters and sawdust in his hair and a six-inch piece of barbwire dangling from his chin. When Miss Mobley asked him what had happened, he had said something like, "I tripped and fell over the fence while I was walking to school this morning." Yeah, right. Like he could really fool anyone with that story.

No, Hambone Oxcart was no ordinary fifth grader. I'd rather eat hash browns every day for lunch for the rest of my life than have to stand up to his wrath.

Six hours later, I squatted on the playground, playing marbles with my friends. The mood was bad, real bad. I couldn't help but show my frustration from my little run-in with Hambone.

"I heard he almost pounded you this morning," Radar Munsky said, chewing noisily on a granola bar.

I didn't say anything as I shot my bull basher into the pile, scattering the marbles.

"He almost pounds everyone, every day, Radar," Snow Cone said.

"Can you believe he charges six dollars now? That's like two months' allowance," Whiz griped. "How am I supposed to afford rubber sheets when Hambone keeps taking my savings?"

All this talk of Hambone was becoming a distraction. I needed to focus. Recess was my only time to practice my marble game, and the tri-state tournament was in two weeks. No point in trying to be modest, I was one of the best marble champions at Pordunce Elementary, but if I had to continue paying Hambone all of my money, I would never be able to afford the entry fee.

I yelled out in frustration and flung my bull basher as hard as I could, right at the center of the pile. What happened next would be the defining moment in my short elementary career. I shot the most amazing shot ever seen at Pordunce Elementary School. My genuine red and gold bull basher hit the center with such a force that it sent all the other marbles flying in every direction. Everyone cheered so loudly I was sure they would give me a new name. Basher, Marble Man, or even King Pordunce would suffice.

But instead of dubbing me an honorary member of the round table of great ones, everyone started looking for their lost marbles. I was so disappointed until I looked and saw my bull basher was missing as well. Oh, I couldn't have that. That marble had cost me dearly in last year's great three-way trade when Tunafish Marrero, Butter Bibowski, and I had swapped our most prized possessions.

I gave up my gerbil and a railroad spike I found in the woods while camping with my dad. In turn, I walked home with a handful of blue-colored robin's eggs and the bull basher. Most kids thought I had lost out, especially when after a month none of the robin's eggs had hatched. The bull basher, however, had proven to be one of the most coveted items at Pordunce Elementary. Marrero never realized he had given me a marble with such famed history. Legend has it my bull basher was made from the broken pieces of a stained glass window from St. Ernieham's Cathedral. You know, the one that burned down three years ago. It's a sure shot, a marble shooter's dream. I knew I simply had to find it before some kid tucked it away in his pocket.

I started looking in the taller weeds and after several minutes, I finally found it stuck under a very large rock. When I looked up, I was all alone on the playground. All the other kids had headed in to get ready for the buses. At least, I thought I was alone. That was until Hambone's fat cockroach, Phil, came scurrying out from underneath the rock where my basher had landed.

No one, other than Hambone, had ever been alone with Phil. From where I was standing, Phil could have easily passed as a small cat. He was hissing, of course, as most mammoth cockroaches do, but in between hisses, I swear I heard him say, "Hashbrown, give me that marble!"

I looked around, trying to see where that voice had come from. Someone must have been hiding in the trees.

"Give it to me!" The voice hissed. Phil's lips didn't move because he didn't have any, but I most certainly heard him talking.

I swallowed. "My marble? What do you want with my marble?" Things had just gotten weird. Don't get me wrong, I'm sure animals chat all the time with each other—I've seen it on television—but Phil didn't have hands. What was he going to do with my marble?

"What I do with the marble is my business. Now give it to me or else!" Phil was not messing around. Just as he finished hissing at me, he began scurrying quickly in my direction.

I was terrified. I didn't have time to think out a reasonable plan. My marble-instinct took over. I really don't remember winding up, but before I had a chance to say Quezie-shmezie—

Splat!

I didn't even wait around to say any final words over Phil, I just ran. I ran as fast as my red and white sneakers allowed, leaving my bull basher in what would be its final resting space. Smack dab in the puddle of goop that was once a cockroach—Hambone's cockroach.

Chapter 3
We're Not Talking Ketchup

There I stood, hiding next to the vending machines, disguised as a potted plant. I brushed the plastic leaves from my face and stared down the hallway toward the front double doors. Snow Cone always said this ridiculous costume would come in handy one day.

"Come on, Mom, move that minivan," I whispered. I had to be cautious. "Be cool, Hashbrown," I told myself. Fifteen minutes had passed since the last student left for the buses, but I wasn't about to take any chances. Not with my life hanging in the balance. "You're such an idiot," I said to myself. Why did instinct always take over when I had a marble in my hand? It was a curse, not a gift.

Leaning forward, I peered around the corner just as the sound of footsteps echoed down the hallway. Was this it? Could this be *him*? Was I about to be pulverized by Hambone while wearing an emergency disguise I had just pulled from my locker?

Relief swept over me, when Mr. Hackerbits, the half-deaf, half-blind school janitor appeared, dragging along his mop bucket. I watched the janitor bump into a locker, splashing his mop water across the floor. *Was that shampoo?*

I sniffed the air. It was no mystery the janitor couldn't read labels and often used hair care products for his routine cleanings. He must've noticed the unusual plant standing next to the vending machines. Leaning in close, he examined me through squinting eyes. I held my breath, but I guess it wasn't necessary. I could've made armpit noises, and Mr. Hackerbits wouldn't have noticed. After scratching his head, the janitor squirted my face with a bottle of window cleaner and disappeared into a classroom.

"Tropical punch," I said, licking my lips. "That explains the flies on all the windows."

The sight of a lemon-colored minivan pulled into view. "It's about time." I quickly stepped out of the flowerpot. "Here goes nothing." I took off at an all-out sprint, bursting down the hallway as fast as my stems could go. If anyone other than the janitor had happened to glance down that hall, they would have seen a large bush running with lightning speed.

"Hey, Hashbrown," my mom said, opening the van door. I dove into my seat and poked my head just barely above the windowsill. "What's with the plant costume? Are you in a school play?"

"Just drive, Mom. Just drive," I said.

Half an hour later, I sat in my tree house scribbling down my last will and testament. By the following morning, I was as good as dead. Hambone Oxcart, the number one bully at Pordunce Elementary School, was out for blood, Hashbrown blood—and we're not talking ketchup. I yelped as a knock rang out on my tree house's trapdoor.

"Since when do we lock this?" Snow Cone's voice drifted up from beneath the floor.

"What took you so long?" I asked, helping him through the trapdoor.

Snow Cone grinned. "What are you talking about? I just got off the bus. Speaking of which, why were you a no-show?"

I rose to my feet and stared out the window. "Did anyone say anything about me on the bus?" I asked.

"No. Why?"

"We've been best friends for a long time, haven't we?" I sat back down and looked at my pal.

"Since diapers," Snow Cone said with a smile.

"Yeah, and if ever I were in a pickle, you'd always be there for me, right?"

Snow Cone blinked. "Uh-huh."

"So what if I was to tell you . . . I'd gotten myself into a nasty dill pickle with pimentos?" I gnawed on my cheek as I watched Snow Cone try to crack the code.

"Pimentos?" he asked, chuckling and scratching his head. "You mean you flooded your living room with tapioca pudding?"

"No, Snow Cone," I said shaking my head. "I said piment-os . . ."

Snow Cone laughed harder. "I think my secret language skills are a little rusty. I'm not sure I know what pimentos means anymore."

"Yeah you do," I said.

"Well, that's just silly, because that would mean you smashed Hambone's pet cockroach with your bull basher." He looked at me. I could tell he hoped he was wrong.

I just nodded my head and frowned. "What do you think, Snow?"

You could've heard a pin drop had Snow Cone not been screaming.

It took several minutes for him to stop thrashing around the tree house like a freshly caught trout. I gave him a paper sack and watched as he hyperventilated.

"When did . . . this happen?" he asked in between breaths.

"During recess. You could've stopped me if you hadn't gone in so fast to catch the bus."

"Oh right, now it's my fault you've gone mental?" Snow crumpled the paper sack and tossed it in the corner.

"No, this is my fault, but I don't know what I'm supposed to do. I'm too young to die."

"Plus, the tree house isn't completely finished," Snow said. "You've got at least another month before it'll be ready for satellite network."

I rolled my eyes. "Thanks, Snow, you're the best."

"This type of emergency calls for all members of the club to be on red alert." Snow Cone dropped down the tree house ladder to raise the alarm. Within twenty minutes, the tree house had filled up with my most trusted comrades, but not one of them had a clue of what I should do.

Whiz Peterson wet his pants, twice.

Bubblegum Bulkins swallowed so harshly, he coughed up a three-year-old piece of Double Trouble bubble gum and started smacking his lips.

Measles Mumphrey said he thought he had come down with the measles for the fourth time. But he had no choice but to stay in the tree house because Four Hips Dixon got stuck in the trap door trying to sneak his way out.

What was I to do? There were six of us, and we were not by any means the runts of the class. Four Hips alone carried his lunch to school in a tuba case. But I knew I couldn't ask them to fight this fight. Not with Hambone. They had their whole lives ahead of them. I really didn't have much of a choice.

As the great Einstein Bafferty said, just before he came

down with mono and his family moved to Pittsburg: "When the going gets tough, its time to pack your stuff."

I had to jump town and fast.

I quickly gave everyone assignments. Whiz got on the phone and checked the price of bus tickets to Alaska. Bubblegum went over my finances, which didn't take long. If only I hadn't wasted my last dollar on those ten bouncy balls last week that all got lost in one terrific bounce. Stupid impulse buy. I would have to forget about the bus.

Four Hips went to the tree house refrigerator and busted out the emergency supply of brain-numbing ice pops. They made a great snack, plus they really worked at giving you ideas. The problem was trying to wrestle one free from Four Hips.

"Four Hips, give me one of those," Bubblegum said.

"But I already called dibs on the box," Four Hips said, hugging the package of ice pops like it was his favorite teddy bear.

"You can't call dibs on the whole box." Amazingly enough, Bubblegum managed to pry a cantaloupe ice pop from Four Hips's death grip. Four Hips generally didn't put up much of a fight for any reason. Unless, of course, it was over food, in which case, all bets were off. No one could forget that dreadful Saturday two years ago when Four Hips dropped a half-eaten chocolate bar into the polar bear cages at the zoo. The cross-eyed bear is now the zoo's main attraction.

Measles rummaged through our supply stash to pack me a survival kit: two pieces of sturdy string, a calculator watch, a gas mask, a rubber-band ball, a bug-watching book, a handful of bottle rockets, and silly putty.

"Great guys," I said. "Now how do I put this stuff to good use? Silly putty? Are you serious, Measles?"

"Oh sure, make fun of my survival kit, if that'll make you feel better," Measles's lips chattered around a large piece of cranberry ice pop. "Why, Hashbrown? Why now? Of all the days you could've picked to turn loony, why did you pick this one, to cross, Hambone? It's my birthday this Friday. What about the party?" Measles almost began to cry.

We would just have to let him believe that. I didn't have time to jog Measles's memory again.

"You do realize Hambone Oxcart's the most feared bully ever to walk down the halls of Pordunce," Bubblegum said, smacking his head with his hand.

"Remember what happened to that one kid, what's his name? The one from the dodgeball accident." Whiz was hopping back and forth trying to keep from whizzing.

"That was no accident," Snow Cone said. "We tried to tell him to commit dodgeball suicide like the rest of us, but he didn't hear us. Poor guy never even had a nickname, and now no one really knows what his real name was. The word on the streets is he's being homeschooled and forced to drink most of his meals through a straw."

I tapped my foot anxiously against the tree house floor. "None of this is helping you know."

"Hastbown, mamy ooh can thay you thorry," said Four Hips. His tongue and lips were swollen and turquoise in color from the three mystery berry ice pops he had shoved in his mouth.

"Thay I'm thorry?" I mimicked. "You're kidding, right? You want me to say I'm sorry to the kid Fibber saw pinning Mr. Buse against the lockers and taking *his* lunch money. Linebacker Buse who played on a professional football team before injuring his leg kicking the quarterback!"

"You mean the sixth grade social studies teacher?"

"The same."

"Oh yeah, that would be bad, I guess," said Four Hips.

"Come on guys, think." I was losing my cool. I hadn't even had a chance to get my affairs in order, and soon the sun would be setting. The club would have to go in for the night, leaving me all alone with my thoughts.

A knock rang out on the trap door. We all froze. I quickly counted all the bodies in the tree house. We were all there. Who could be knocking on the trapdoor?

"Don't answer it," Measles whispered, several brand-new pustules springing to life on his forehead.

"You don't think . . . ?" Snow Cone asked, looking at me. I shook my head. No, it was impossible. Hambone didn't know where I lived. I was very careful to cover my tracks, and besides I was pretty sure his parents tethered him to a pole right after school.

"Who . . . who is it?" I asked in my gruffest voice. I was going for old and ornery, hoping whoever it was would just assume a bunch of angry men were hanging out in the tree house.

"It's me, Saddle Bags," a familiar voice drifted up from beneath the wood.

"Saddle Bags Bollinger?" Four Hips asked, his voice quivering.

"The one and only," Saddle Bags answered.

I carefully propped the trapdoor open and peered down. Sure enough, the massive girth of Saddle Bags blocked my view of the ground below. "What do you want?"

"Uh, hello? We're here for tryouts," Saddle Bags said, swaying to the side to give me a look at the large line of my classmates stretching down the sidewalk.

Snow Cone slapped me on the back. "Today is club house tryouts," he said.

"That's today?" I asked.

Whiz nodded his head excitedly. "Yeah, of course. You had us pass out flyers last week."

Joining my clubhouse had risen to the top of Pordunce Elementary School's priority list since we held a seminar last spring. I gave a fantastic workshop on how to deliver award-winning performances during show and tell. It was so good that the following Friday Measles, heeding my advice, actually convinced Ms. Pinkens that the cow patty he had plucked from a field was in fact an authentic organic Frisbee. I get teary-eyed every time I think about it.

"So do I get to come up or what?" Saddle Bags asked. "I don't think this ladder's gonna hold me much longer."

It was the worst time to be holding tryouts, especially with Hambone on the warpath. "I'm sorry, everyone," I shouted down from the trapdoor. "We're going to have to postpone tryouts for another date." The yard instantly filled with groaning voices. Several students chucked their show and tell projects to the ground in disgust. "I'm really sorry."

"Who does he think he is?" came a voice from somewhere in the middle of the crowd. "Calling us out here like this and then postponing it!" The line of students shuffled out of my yard, and I latched the trap door closed.

"That's a huge setback," Snow Cone said, scribbling down some notes on a clipboard. "You're going to have some explaining to do at the pep rally."

"I'll make it up to them somehow, but I can't worry about that right now," I said, covering my eyes with my palms.

Bubblegum's eyes perked up. "Hey, what if we pulled the old Pamplona Pinch. That hasn't been done since the third grade."

Snow Cone looked up at me. "Not bad, it could work."

The Pamplona Pinch was a gimmick we pulled two

years ago to rid ourselves of another bully, Gorilla Gomez, who was almost as bad as Hambone. We convinced him they were holding auditions for the running of the bulls at my Uncle Homer's ranch in Wyoming. After explaining to him that the prize was equal to an entire year's worth of lunch money and giving him a fake map, Gomez disappeared into the mountains.

Oh, don't worry; I'm sure he's fine. To this day, Wyoming has the largest number of Big Foot sightings in North America.

"No," I shook my head. "Remember, Hambone doesn't like words typed on paper, and he'll never fall for it if we write it in crayon."

Over the next five minutes, each of my friends tried their best to contribute ideas.

Measles suggested I pull a "Pyro Muffin" but we no longer had a giant opossum costume available.

Whiz mentioned the possibility of doing a fake funeral, but embalming fluid has always made me nauseous.

"There's always the 'Road Runner Special,' " Four Hips added.

"Oh sure, and where are we going to find a giant anvil this time of year?" It was useless. All of their suggestions were good ideas if we had a month to plan. But I had less than day before Hambone came a-knocking.

Suddenly the sound of sweet music floated up from the sidewalk. "Oh, Flinton?" It was Misty Piccolo, the most beautiful girl at Pordunce Elementary.

I mentioned before that nobody called me by my first name? Well, I make an exception for one person and one person only and that's Misty Piccolo. Not even my own mother calls me Flinton. Misty was her real name *and* her nickname because that's what it felt like whenever she walked into a room. Misty. I nervously stuck my head out of the window and smiled down at her.

"There you are, Flinton. Did you forget about our science project?"

The science project. It was the happiest day of my life when Ms. Pinkens partnered me with Misty Piccolo for our end of term science project. What were the odds of it happening to me? How could I have forgotten the science project? Maybe the fact that I had a date with death tomorrow in front of the whole school was a valid reason.

"No, Misty, I haven't forgotten. I'll be down in a minute," I answered Misty, the vision of beauty, and pulled myself away from the window.

"I sound like a girl," I said, my cheeks turning red.

Everyone was grinning at me. "No, Misty, I haven't forgotten," they mocked.

I felt the redness in my cheeks turn to purple. "Go on, laugh it up, but tomorrow I'm going to tell Hambone I traded the basher to you, Bulkins."

Bubblegum Bulkins swallowed dryly and his eyes grew to the size of kumquats. "But I wasn't even laughing at you, Hashbrown. I . . . I just remembered something funny from earlier." He had strawberry rhubarb ice pop dribbling out of his nose.

"Yeah right. Anyways, I've got to go work on my science project with Misty."

"That's it, Hashbrown!" Snow Cone shouted.

"What's it?"

"The answer to your problem with Hambone."

Finally, Snow had come through. I knew I could trust him. "Well, what is it?" I asked anxiously.

"Misty Piccolo. She's the answer."

Oh man, he had lost it. This whole Hambone thing

had probably pushed him over the edge. I blame myself, of course. After all, if it weren't for my stupidity, Snow Cone would've been perfectly fine and not mental.

"Snow, I don't think Misty Piccolo is going to fight Hambone for me. That's ridiculous." Misty *was* freakishly tall. She towered over us by at least a foot, but she was a girl, and Hambone was, well you know, a hippo.

"That's not what I meant." Snow gave me a withering look. "Think about it for a second. Misty Piccolo . . ." Snow's voice trailed off as he tried to make everyone understand, but it wasn't working. No one in the room had any idea what he was talking about. It became so quiet in the tree house, the only thing that could be heard was the muffled sound of Four Hips' stomach digesting twelve ice pops.

Whiz exploded from the far corner of the room with excitement. He didn't even care that he'd wet himself again, which was really not a shock. (Whiz's bladder was the size of an acorn—a modern medical mystery.) He hopped around and waved his hand frantically in the air, waiting for someone to call on him. We all knew Whiz wasn't supposed to get too excited. His mother made it very clear if he didn't stop getting riled up, she was going to make him start wearing a barrel to school.

"Yes, Whiz, what is it?" I asked, stifling my laughter.

"Tony Ten Fingers! Tony Ten Fingers!" Whiz shouted.

Immediately everyone dropped to the floor and became as quiet as we possibly could.

"Where?" Measles whispered, terrified of the possibility Tony Ten Fingers was near by.

"No, not here." Whiz giggled. "Tony Ten Fingers is Misty Piccolo's half-cousin." The light suddenly went on in each of our heads. Maybe not in Four Hips' head. He was too busy gathering up the pieces of the four hard-boiled eggs that he'd crushed when he fell to the floor.

Snow Cone smiled. "Exactly. Good work, Whiz."

Of course! Tony Ten Fingers of the sixth grade Figanewty Family, the toughest organization in the entire school. The Figanewty Family was run by Cordovo Figanewty who moved into town two years ago from New York City. Tony was his right hand man. Overall, there were about fifteen members of the organization, and Tony Ten Fingers was the meanest of the bunch. There were only rumors how he got his name. Something about accidentally sticking his fingers in a meat grinder, which broke the machine, but amazingly all of his fingers were still attached.

He was one tough cookie. I'd be willing to bet Tony Ten Fingers alone could put up a good fight with Hambone, but it wasn't necessary. Tony was so powerful, because of his connection with Cordovo Figanewty, who, with just the snap of his fingers, could have even Ms. Borfish swinging her mangled spatula at Hambone.

No one really knew where Cordovo got all his money and his power. Every day he strolled into school wearing flashy pinstriped sweat suits and spotless white sneakers. In lunch, when the rest of the school was forced to eat meat loaf and cabbage stew, Cordovo Figanewty dined on prime rib and a baked potato. And when the other students had to wash down that mush with day-old chocolate milk, Cordovo swigged Pineapple Slurp from a long-stemmed crystal glass. Cordovo had the connections. . . . No, he *was* the connection. And Misty Piccolo, that sweet vision of beauty, was my way in. Snow Cone was a genius.

"I don't get it," Four Hips whispered. "What's so brilliant about that criminal Tony Ten Fingers?"

"It's not just Tony Ten Fingers, Four Hips, it's the Figanewty Family," Snow Cone explained. "If we could somehow convince them to protect Hashbrown, then we could save his life."

"Yeah, I've heard of at least four or five different people in school who were offered protection from the Figanewty Family," I added.

"I think Misty Piccolo will help you out if you ask her. My brother, Kibbles, told me Misty owns the only soft spot in Tony's heart," Bubblegum said.

"But you don't have anything Hashbrown, just this dumb ol' survival kit. What can you give to Cordovo Figanewty that will make him want to protect you?" Measles had begun to itch anxiously at his neck.

He had a point. I sighed with frustration. "Look, I don't have a choice, do I? Sometime tomorrow, Hambone is going to find me and when he does, I'm patty-cakes. I want to live to see my next birthday and to do that I need Mr. Figanewty. I have to try, otherwise I'm doomed."

"Hashbrown's right," Snow Cone agreed. "Now we've got a few minutes before we have to go home. We'll work on a good plan for tomorrow while you go down and get Misty to set up an appointment with Cordovo."

Easier said then done. Misty Piccolo was the girl of my dreams. I heard bells whenever she entered the room, partly because she wore them on her shoelaces, but that's beside the point. Whenever I found myself trapped in a conversation with her, I ended up sounding like a stuttering monkey. I slapped myself across the face. "Pull it together," I whispered. Maybe, just maybe, I would be able to muster up a sentence. If not, I suspected tomorrow there could be mashed hash browns on the lunch menu.

Chapter 4
The Wonderful Misty Piccolo

I made my way down the eight wooden steps of my tree house ladder, trying to gather my wits. There she was, sitting cross-legged on the sidewalk with her face buried in the latest copy of *Rain Wilmo, the Superstar Superhero* comic book. The afternoon sunrays glistened off her perfectly fashioned hairdo. A family of birds perched on a tall branch of the tree right above her head began singing the lovely song, "Breeze in the Meadows." I watched her read for several moments, my heart racing.

But then the bird song quickly changed into the funeral march, and my feet began to work properly.

"So Flinton, I was wondering what you were thinking we should do for this project. I've never gotten anything less than an A+ on an assignment, but this one seems to be a little tricky." Misty set aside the magazine and stared dreamily into my eyes. Oh, those eyes. Her sparkle-covered eyelids fluttered like butterflies in a gentle breeze. I may have understood two whole words of her sentence. Everything else blurred together in my ears.

"Uh . . . the project. Um . . . we should do the project, and . . . and get an A," I stammered, losing focus for a moment. Did I just rephrase what she said? What was I trying to say? It was a mystery.

Misty giggled, but then gasped. "Oh my, is that blood on your leg?" She pointed.

It was possible. Buck-toothed armadillos could've attacked me on my way down the tree house ladder and I wouldn't have noticed. As I glanced down, I saw the remains of a popsicle stick stuck to my pants. Throughout the entire ruckus happening in the tree house I had probably rolled over an ice pop.

"Oh that? That's just nothing," I said. I shifted, trying to act cool.

"I was thinking maybe we could take your ant farm you displayed in show and tell a month ago and build them a mini shopping mall. We could take notes on which ants are better at accessorizing," she said. Misty was very excited about this idea. I didn't have the heart to tell her that just last week, Snow Cone and I destroyed the ant farm re-enacting an alien invasion with a handful of grasshoppers and a package of firecrackers. I needed to change the subject.

"I'm in big trouble, Misty, and I need your help!" I belched out. There, of course, were more proper ways to address that issue. I could have taken my time, perhaps even struck up some conversation before dropping the painful news of my imminent death on the sweet Misty Piccolo. But, never being one to beat around the bush, I quickly blurted out my words. I was pleased with the outcome.

"What?" Misty said. "What do you mean you're in trouble, Flinton?"

It took me the next fifteen minutes to clue Misty in on what I had done and more importantly, where she fit into the equation. I felt sweaty under my eyeballs, behind my ears and under my leg pits.

"Are you sure Hambone's that mean?" Misty asked. "He seems so quiet."

"Trust me. Without a doubt," I answered.

"Yeah, but I don't think there's any proof he was the one that collapsed Jerky Bridge last year. I think it was because of the earthquake."

"Don't believe everything you hear on the news, Misty. Fibber Mckenzie said he saw . . . whatever." I tried to remain calm. "The fact is Hambone is going to pound me into pizza dough if I don't get help."

"I don't know, Flinton, Tony's been very busy lately. They've taken over quite a few paper routes this past month, not to mention all the time he spends at the laundromat. You would think his clothes were never clean." Misty smiled and stared up at the evening sky. "Oh look, Flinton, it's the sunset."

I looked over my shoulder at the sun slowly sliding behind the horizon. It very well could have been a giant hash brown dropping into a fiery vat of cooking oil. "Misty, you've got to try. All I need is a few minutes of Mr. Figanewty's time, that's it. Please!"

Let's be honest. A few minutes of Mr. Figanewty's time were not easy to come by. Even if I did manage to score a meeting with the don of Pordunce elementary, I still needed something to buy some protection from the family. Misty's part in all of this was very small.

"Oh, all right, I'll see what I can do, but I'm not making any promises." Misty got to her feet and brushed the gravel off of her skirt. I stood as well and frowned. I could barely see above her shoulders. Why did girls have to grow like mutant zucchini plants? I had failed to make a mark with the yard stick on the kitchen wall for almost eight months now. I was beginning to fear my growing was completely done. At least there was always horse racing.

I looked up at my house, and my stomach lurched. There was my mother standing on the front porch holding my dinosaur pajamas.

"Its pj time, Hashbrown. Let's get a move on," My mom held out the embarrassing pieces of clothing and almost lost them in the night breeze. I began to wonder how bad it really would be to get flattened by Hambone.

Misty giggled. "Pj time, Flinton?"

"Yeah, well . . . uh . . . sha . . . I always help my mom put the rest of the kiddies in their pajamas. Don't know how she would do it without me," I said with an awkward grin. "So, uh, I'd better get going."

"I'll call you later with what Tony tells me." Misty strolled down the sidewalk, a wild gazelle prancing in the dusk.

Later that night, I waited by the telephone. She would call. She had to call. Just before my mother came in, giving me the last five minutes before lights out, the phone rang. I dove across the bed and plucked it off the receiver before anyone else had a chance to answer it.

It was Misty.

"Hello, Flinton." Even over the phone her voice sounded dreamy.

"Hey, Misty . . . any good news?" my voice cracked.

"Well . . ." That didn't sound like a good "well," more like an it-was-nice-knowing-you "well." I nearly dropped the phone. "Well, Tony told me to tell you tomorrow isn't a good day for the family. He said there were a few, so to speak, legal issues Mr. Figanewty had to attend to. He said he might be able to squeeze you into an appointment some-time around . . . next September."

"September!" I screamed. "I can't wait until next

September! I'll have a full grown tulip on my grave by then."

"You didn't let me finish, Flinton," Misty said. "I told him it absolutely had to be tomorrow and I would be very upset if he couldn't do this little favor for me."

"And? What did he say?" The anticipation was killing me.

"11:45, tomorrow, in the teacher's lounge. Come alone and, um . . . Tony said for your sake, you had better have something worth Mr. Figanewty's time." She giggled. "Whatever that means. He's so silly sometimes."

"Thank you, Misty. I owe you big time." I swallowed in relief.

"Just make sure we get an A+ on this science project, Flinton. That's all." With that, the sweet sound of Misty's voice left the other end of the receiver, leaving me alone to think about tomorrow's plan. Boy, did I ever need it to be a good one.

Chapter 5
Thus Sayeth the Oracle

The next day at school, Snow Cone, Whiz, and I cut through the hallways carefully avoiding the more obvious hangouts of our nemesis, Hambone. These were the janitorial closet and any place where you could find wood chips. Hambone loved nibbling on wood chips. There was a weird feeling floating around the halls at Pordunce Elementary. It was almost as if every student had an idea of what was about to happen to me. Several second graders passed us but avoided making eye contact. I had to ignore this.

During the night I'd had a nightmare, one much worse than dancing hash browns. Hambone was in it, wearing a muumuu and juggling roast beef sandwiches. I also saw my aunt Morphie playing checkers with a stuffed goat. When I awoke I was covered with sweat and there was the faint smell of horseradish in the air. It was a clear message. I would not survive the showdown with Hambone. I pushed the thoughts of my upcoming death from my mind and redoubled my focus on the game plan.

That morning on the school bus, Snow Cone debriefed me on what he and the others had decided. To have even a spitter's chance of surviving a meeting with Cordovo

Figanewty, I needed to find something of value. No matter how hard they tried, none of my friends could come up with anything worth the mafia's time. It was then, after their brain picking session, that they'd decided I needed to visit the Oracle.

"I've got a bad feeling about this, guys," Whiz whispered as we rounded the corner into the third grade wing. "The Oracle's a real nutso."

On most occasions, Snow Cone and I carried out all of our necessary tasks together. The rest of my crew generally waited out at our fallback location, Mrs. Marrazat's Arts and Crafts closet, to find out how things went. Today, however, was an exception to our normal routine; one needing extra precautions. We brought Whiz along for an alibi. Every teacher at Pordunce Elementary knew of Whiz's bladder problem. If some annoying teacher became too nosy about what we were doing out of class, Whiz just waved his golden hall pass, and we were in the clear.

"Look, we don't like this any more than you, but the Oracle's the real deal," I said.

I understood why Whiz got a little wary whenever we entered the third-grade wing. It brought back many bad memories. It had been two and a half years since the dreaded Slip and Slide Hallway Tumble incident that sent Vice Principal Humidor and six unsuspecting third graders to the hospital. Snow Cone had told Whiz not to drink that sixty-four once traveling mug full of citrus soda. And why Whiz had decided on that day to carry his two-year collection of jawbreakers around with him for show and tell, I'll never know. But bad memories or no, I needed to talk with the Oracle, and that led me to the third-grade wing and locker number 366.

Gabriel Yucatan, otherwise known as the Oracle, had

been stuck in locker 366 ever since a couple of sixth grade bullies crammed him in there seven years ago. He was always a bit on the cautious side when it came to his locker, which was the reason he changed his combination three times a day. During a routine combination switch, the bullies had surprised him from behind and locked him in his locker before he had a chance to finish the change.

Tons of people tried to help him out, but it was too late. After Corporal Kitna, the militant substitute DARE representative got spooked by an anonymous phone call, the lockers at Pordunce had been newly remodeled with tank armor. They were impossible to break open. Gabriel had been living inside his ever since.

"You've gotta feel sorry for him," Snow Cone said, as we approached the ominous locker.

"I don't," I said. "It's not that bad of a gig. After all, he charges for his predictions. I also heard he managed to dig himself a maze of tunnels with the use of plastic spoons. How else would he know what's going on throughout the school?"

"All right, Hashbrown," Snow Cone said, pointing at the locker. "You're up."

"Guys, I don't know about this anymore," Whiz said, taking a step back and away from the locker. "I got a funny feeling."

Snow and I chuckled.

"Not that sort of feeling!" Whiz shouted.

We all knew what sort of funny feelings Whiz got, and they usually involved wet pants.

"Look, this is the only way to find out what Hashbrown needs," said Snow Cone.

"Yeah, but this guy creeps me out."

"He creeps everybody out," I said. "What do you expect

from a guy who has lived in a locker well into his high school years?"

"Is it true, what they say about him?" Whiz asked, lowering his voice. "That he has red eyes and his fingernails have grown so long he pokes kids in the ears out from the locker vent?"

"No, that's not true," Snow Cone said. "That's all a bunch of—ouch!" Snow Cone grabbed the back of his ear and spun around. We all spun around just in time to see locker 366 trembling. "He poked me!"

"If you don't mind, I'd appreciate it if you move along down the hall," an eerie voice echoed out deep within the locker. The three of us fell silent and eyed each other warily.

"Er, sorry, Gabriel, we were just—"

"I don't answer to that name anymore. I am the all-seeing Oracle and you're impeding my view of the hallway. I'm missing all the action."

"But nothing's going on right now. The morning bell has already rung. All the kids have gone to class," I said, squinting and imagining a ghostly figure with red eyes and ridiculously long finger nails lurking behind the locker door. "Besides, none of us are impeding on anything. Whiz is wearing rubber pants."

"Not im-*pee*-ding, I said impeding," the Oracle sighed. "It means to block, hinder, or obstruct. In other words, unless you intend to pay, get out of my way."

"This guy's good," whispered Snow Cone.

"Of course, I'm good, I am the Oracle. Now, follow the summoning ritual, and I'll grant you my predictions."

Reluctantly, I approached the locker and followed the age-old ritual of summoning the Oracle. When performed correctly, the summoning ritual was quite amazing. The

Oracle was very particular about how one was to call him. First, the person in need of predictions, in this case me, had to knock very firmly on the locker six times, no more, no less. Secondly, I had to squeal like a pig and then say "Boondoggle, boondoggle, boondoggle" while running in place and flapping my arms like a chicken. Lastly, I was to cram my payment through the locker vent and wait for an approving moan from the Oracle. In this case, I'd brought forty-five nickels, a frozen microwaveable pepperoni pizza, and a 2002 Rip Strapinski baseball card—a standard requirement.

"Why does he always want a Rip Strapinski baseball card?" Whiz asked, staring at the card as we passed it through the locker slots. "He must have a million of them by now. I don't even think Rip Strapinski's played in a major league game."

"Silence, you fiend!" the Oracle boomed, sounding more like a second-rate Dracula impersonator. "You must never insult the wondrous Rip Strapinski!"

I threw my hands up in disgust. "Great, Whiz. Have you forgotten everything we told you before coming here?"

"Yeah, Whiz," Snow Cone said. "You must never talk bad about Rip Strapinski. According to the Oracle, Rip is supposed to make the most important discovery ten years from now and lead the Oracle out of his locker prison and into a land of fortune."

"What's the discovery?" Whiz asked.

"It is a secret you imbecile," the Oracle shouted again. This was not going as planned. Not too many students were dumb enough to annoy the Oracle. "Now, I have accepted your payment. Say what it is you wish to know and be gone."

Whiz and Snow Cone looked at me, and I nodded

my head quickly. "I don't know if you know this already or not, but I am in a bit of stink. I accidentally smashed Hambone's—"

The Oracle chuckled. "Accidentally? I'd say not. From what I witnessed, it was no accident," he said in between his laughter.

I scrunched up my face. "But how could you have seen that?" I asked. I had been at this school for over four years now. I knew for a fact there weren't any lockers on the playground.

"Never mind that," the Oracle said. "Continue."

"Anyways, I need protection from Hambone, and I have a meeting with Cordovo Figanewty. If I don't come up with something to pay him, I'm going to have even bigger problems."

"Silence," the Oracle said. "I will now tell you what you need to know."

The three of us waited and listened. Several minutes passed in silence. The anticipation was killing me. I had to know what to do, and, clearly, it was not going to be easy. Soon, the sound of a microwave heating up began to hum and the smell of frozen pizza reheating wafted from the locker slots.

"Do you think he forgot about us?" Whiz asked above the obnoxious sound of the Oracle munching on his meal. I shrugged. After almost ten minutes of no response, Snow spotted a tiny white piece of paper as it shot through the slot and floated gently to the ground.

The Oracle had spoken.

Whiz scrambled to the floor and plucked up the small message.

"What does it say?" I asked.

Whiz's eyes darted across the paper. "It says $2.00 off

our next diaper purchase." Whiz looked excitedly up at us, but then appeared confused. "What the? Hey! What do you mean by that?" he shouted, kicking at the locker. "I don't need diapers."

"Whiz, the message is written on the back," Snow Cone said.

Whiz flipped the paper over. His eyes grew big with alarm. Slowly, he turned the message so I could read the two words written on the back of the coupon:

Bull Basher

"My bull basher?" I blurted out. "But how? It's resting in a crater that was once a talking cockroach." I couldn't believe it. *This* was the great wisdom of the Oracle? "What a crock of stew!" I shouted furiously.

"Do not mock my vision," the Oracle answered.

"But what if Hambone has already taken my marble? What then?"

The Oracle was silent.

"Come on, let's get out of here," Snow Cone said, urging me along. Whiz seemed eager to go as well, and the Oracle would speak no more on the matter.

"Fine," I said. Apparently, the only thing worth Cordovo Figanewty's time would have to be my bull basher. Everything else would just leave me with a new set of sneakers, ones made of concrete. I seriously doubted the marble would still be there, but I had no other choice. Crumpling up the message, I tossed it to the floor as we walked away from the Oracle's locker.

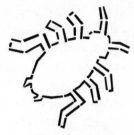

Chapter 6

Hambone's Discovery

"So we stick to the plan, agreed?" I asked Snow as I met up with him after first period English with Mr. Coppercork.

"Agreed, but are you sure it's wise for you to go alone to the playground?" Snow Cone was not convinced sending his best friend to the crime scene without a bodyguard was the best idea.

"Snow, there's no way any of our teachers will give us both hall passes. They know our history too well." Every teacher in the school knew giving us both hall passes at the same time pretty much resulted in a catastrophe whether intentional or not. Last year, Principal Herringtoe added that clause in his welcome packet to new teachers. It was too risky not to.

"Yeah, but, Hashbrown, I'm a little worried," Snow Cone replied emptying his pockets of gum wrappers into the trash cash next to the school supply store. "We haven't even spotted Hambone yet, which makes me believe he could be roaming around outside."

The school store was in fact nothing more than an unused janitorial closet with a small selection of pencils, erasers, composition notebooks, and folders hanging from pegs on the back wall of the closet. There was a rusty metal folding chair propped against the open closet door.

Operating the store was a burly, female fourth grader wearing jelly shoes and sporting an unhealthy number of plastic barrettes in her hair. She clutched a bank deposit bag bulging with crumpled one-dollar bills at her waist. Luinda Sharpie, otherwise known throughout the underground amateur wrestling circuit as *The Manatee*, had a crush on Snow Cone. She nervously jabbed the sharpened end of a pencil beneath her braces, adjusting one of the rubber bands that had wiggled loose. She giggled hoarsely, sounding more like a braying donkey than a ten-year-old girl. "Hi, Snow Cone. I like your jacket. Is it new?"

Snow Cone shuddered. "No, I've had this since the second grade. I always wear it."

"It fits you nicely." Her smile widened and the hall light gleamed off her front teeth, temporarily blinding both of us. An awkward silence followed where neither Snow Cone nor I had any clue of how to escape Luinda's enormously bulbous eyeballs.

She motioned behind her at the meager store. "Do you need any folders?"

"No, we're good, Mana . . . I mean Luinda," I said, tugging on Snow Cone's sleeve.

"I've got a great selection of pastel colored Trapper Keepers. They just arrived." She snatched an armful of school supplies and displayed them as if she were an overpaid game show host's assistant.

"Nah, thanks though," Snow Cone muttered.

"Do you want to see me chew a pencil eraser into paste?"

"Um . . . maybe next time," Snow Cone said, "we're pretty busy at the moment."

"Well then, next time it is, Snow," Luinda beamed. We quickly removed ourselves from the shop's queue and hurried down the hallway.

"Why am I the lucky one to have Luinda Sharpie in love with me?" Snow Cone whined. "Why couldn't it be Brandy Newspickle or Shelby Pipercorn?"

I shook my head. I couldn't worry about something as trivial as my best pal's crushes. Right now, we had to focus. Now was the time for survival.

Suddenly the two of us received an awful shock as a giant sixth-grader brushed passed us with a grunt. Luckily, it was just a false alarm. Although known for accidentally launching children into the stratosphere on his favorite playground attraction, Teeter-Totter Williams was mostly harmless.

"Phew," muttered Snow Cone. "That was close."

"Yeah," I agreed. "What we do from now until lunch time is very important. We need to avoid the hallways and the restrooms at all costs. Now, you told the others what they need to do, right?"

"Yeah, yeah, Hashbrown, don't worry." Snow Cone rolled his eyes. "Bubblegum and Measles have already left a trail of wood chips down past the gymnasium."

"And you double checked the gym schedule?" I asked anxiously.

"Of course. Mr. Hemroin's teaching the first graders tether ball, just as we thought."

"Great," I said, pumping my fist. Hambone had never been able to help himself when it came to tether ball. He could stare for hours wondering how the ball never flew away when the kids hit it.

"Four Hips is prepared to act as the human shield so you can sneak into the lunch room," Snow Cone continued, "and Whiz hasn't drunk anything since last night."

I rubbed my hands together. "Good. That's good. I'm gonna make a break for the playground in thirty minutes. That will be just enough time to make sure I don't bump into Hambone on the way out." The plan was set and we quietly ducked into second period science with Ms. Pinkens.

Thirty minutes later, with a hall pass in hand, I sprinted down the hallway toward the playground, praying that somehow my marble was still there.

Pordunce Elementary School was famous for having the absolute worst playground imaginable. Only two of the swings on the swing set worked, both of which usually left a student with rashes in awkward places. (If you're interested in hearing more on that subject, feel free to chat with Rashes Malone. You can usually find him in the nurse's office receiving his cream treatment.) The merry-go-round was square in shape and therefore should've been called a merry-go-nowhere. Of course, if you're feeling lucky, you could always join Teeter-Totter Williams for a ride on the teeter-totter. If you do, be sure to say hello to Astro Anderson when you reach outer space. He's been living on the Russian satellite, Spitnik, for almost six months now.

I was aware of how crummy the playground was. That was why I avoided it at all costs. My normal point of interest was next to the old sandbox, which, because of Ms. Borfish's fifty cats, had been renamed the *clump* box. Not so sure you want to know why.

My marble-playing pals and I had created quite an impressive marble arena, complete with cushioned seats, taken from the six abandoned tractors decorating the grounds, and a very lovely marble washer, which was more or less a fishbowl with paper napkins from the cafeteria. It wasn't much, but to the marble-playing extraordinaire, it was perfect.

I approached the marble hangout quietly, being sure to

search in all directions for anyone who might raise the alarm. The coast was clear. As I stepped into the taller grass where the unfortunate event had occurred less than twenty-four hours ago, I halted.

Phil, the cockroach, was gone.

In the place where he had collapsed after being clobbered by the marble, someone had drawn a very crude chalk outline. There was only one person that would take the time to undergo a complete investigation of the crime scene.

Hambone had been there.

My mind swam frantically. Maybe there was still a chance Hambone Oxcart didn't know I was the culprit. Maybe I could just go back to class, act stupid, and survive the day without a meeting with Cordovo Figanewty. Maybe I was just blowing the whole thing out of proportion. Maybe I— ah, bung fish! Never mind, Hambone knew.

At first I hadn't seen the wooden sign pounded into the ground a few feet away from Phil's chalk drawing. One of the corners of the sign looked as though someone had taken a bite out it. Hambone had taped the bull basher to the post and had written in chalk on the sign three words:

U Dy Hachbran!

Hambone's spelling had actually improved quite a bit. If it weren't for the frightening circumstances, I would've been impressed. Instead, I gulped like a bullfrog. At least Hambone had left the marble. I plucked it off the signpost, my hands trembling. My gamma ray watch, which could actually tell the time on Mars, beeped furiously. It was 10 AM and almost time to change classes.

I gulped again.

My next class was third period math with Miss Mobley. In all of my calculations and planning, I had forgotten one very important piece of information; Hambone was my classmate in third period math.

"Doy!" I exclaimed, cracking the marble against my skull. "I'm such an idiot!" Perhaps someone knew a mathematical equation that could make me invisible. Hambone knew I was guilty. What was to stop him from attacking? It wouldn't be the first time he had done it in a classroom, or actually the forty-first time for that matter. Just last week Hambone had erupted because Miss Mobley confused him with the word *numerator*. He had actually eaten Doberman Dilroy's abacus.

I needed a way to get a hold of Snow Cone. Hopefully, he knew what to do, because now, more than ever, I was in a raspberry jam.

Chapter 7
Jimmy Cracked Corn

The late bell began to ring when I slipped into Miss Mobley's classroom and quietly crept to my seat. There were still many students standing by their desks, jabbering about nonsense. I didn't want to draw any of their attention but unfortunately, I couldn't help myself. As usual, before sitting in my chair, I performed a very unnecessary commando roll.

Of all the things listed in my personal journal of completely idiotic activities to do when facing death, my little somersault in math class quickly soared to the top. Yodeling loudly in a blind gopher's ear and eating a three-week-old tuna fish sandwich out of Hi Mashimoto's locker now tied for second.

All eyes in the classroom fell on me. I was actually surprised to see that a number of the girls were dressed in black and sobbing sadly beneath funeral veils. I never realized how greatly they would miss me. I frantically scanned the classroom in search of Hambone. His desk was still empty, and I collapsed into my seat as relief flooded over me.

"I need to send a message to Snow Cone right now," I whispered under my breath. While Miss Mobley was busy scribbling some garbage about fractions on the chalkboard, I cupped my hands over my mouth and made a piercing whistle with my lips.

The result was immediate. As if summoned from another dimension, Pigeon Criggle appeared at my side. His eyes were wide with excitement. "Reporting to duty, sir!" Pigeon shouted. I cringed. Luckily, a student had stumped Miss Mobley by asking her to explain the meaning of seven-ninths to the class. She hadn't heard Pigeon's announcement.

"Pipe down, Pigeon," I ordered.

"Sir, yes, sir!" Pigeon answered, lowering his voice.

Pigeon was the tiniest first-grader in the entire school. Like so many other of the Pordunce populous who had sprouted their way into the history books, he earned his nickname on his very first day of school when he accidentally missed the bus and over twenty students witnessed a rather mild breeze carry him, backpack and all, the entire way to the school house. Since then, Pigeon had taken up a rather fitting profession of carrying messages throughout the school for an inexpensive payment. He was dying to be accepted in my club and generally carried my messages for free.

"Pigeon, I need you to find Snow Cone and tell him this message." I looked over my shoulder for listeners, relieved to find all of them involved in Miss Mobley's lesson.

"And the message is, sir?" Pigeon asked, his fingers trembling with excitement.

I leaned in closer. "Tell him Donner is Blitzen."

Pigeon blinked his beady eyes in confusion. "The reindeer, sir?" He shook his head. "I don't think I understand. Why would you want to tell. . . ?"

"Pigeon, if you ever want to be in our club you are going

to have to learn when not to ask questions." I didn't have time to explain the particulars of our secret code. Even if I did, I seriously doubted Pigeon with his miniature brain could truly grasp what had taken me and Snow Cone over five years to master. I took a deep breath, calming myself. After all, Pigeon was only a first grader. "Is that understood?"

"Sir, yes, sir!" Pigeon shouted again. This time his voice drew the attention of Miss Mobley, who actually gasped when she saw the teensy first grader hovering a few inches above the ground by my desk.

"Donald Criggle what on earth are you doing in my classroom?" Miss Mobley asked.

Pigeon spun around, flapping his hands and squawking wildly. Before Miss Mobley could grab him, he burst out of the classroom in a cloud of dust that could've easily been mistaken as feathers. I couldn't help myself from laughing. I silently swore that if I ever made it out of this alive I would dub Pigeon an honorary member of the club.

"What was all of that about?" Miss Mobley asked, glaring down at me over her glasses.

I snorted. "Beats me. Pigeon's always popping up like that. You really should lock the door.

"Hmph." Miss Mobley gave me a look and then returned to her lesson.

I learned very little over the course of the next forty-five minutes, not that I ever gathered much from my lessons in Miss Mobley's class. But today all of my concentration was on the classroom door. I believed if I stared long and hard enough the door would remain closed, and Hambone would never appear.

Miss Mobley, on the other hand, started to get on my nerves. I couldn't remember a time throughout the entire year where she had been more interested in what I had to say. Not once did I raise my hand to answer her questions, but for some reason she continually called on me.

"Hashbrown, would you please tell the class what it is you get when you divide one half by three fourths?"

I sighed loudly, rubbing my eyes until they were red. "Um . . . that would be six," I answered, refusing to look away from the door.

"Six what?" Miss Mobley asked in shock.

I flipped through my book. "Uh . . . six apples . . . ma'am," I said. It wasn't my worst response by far.

Miss Mobley snapped her book shut. "I have had it with your attitude," she said. "If you don't intend to pay attention while I am teaching, then there is no point in you being here." This was new. My eyes perked up. "In fact, I have a better idea. Mr. Fidgewarbles is in need of some clean chalkboard erasers. If you hurry, you won't be late for third period. Now go."

Getting permission from Miss Mobley to leave her class for any reason was something that never happened. You could tell just by looking at her hall pass. It was still in its original plastic wrapping for crying out loud. Only Whiz had the green light to go whenever he needed. No one dared stop him in the hallway for fear of stepping in puddles. I knew some greater power had to be at work here. I gave Miss Mobley an odd look.

She in turn responded, "Don't scrunch your face, Hashbrown, you'll get wrinkles." She handed me a paper sack bulging with chalkboard erasers and pointed to the door. "Hurry along now."

Bolting for the door, I almost forgot to gather my stuff. I couldn't leave any evidence, especially my survival kit. I rounded the corner toward the fourth-grade wing when all of a sudden I heard the unmistakable footsteps of something very large approaching. The massive footsteps halted right in front of Miss Mobley's classroom door.

I had to look to be sure, but I needed to use extra stealth. Slowly, I inched my head around the outer edge of the fifth-grade lockers. The massive frame of Hambone breathing heavily in front of the door blocked my view of the vending machines at the end of the hall. Clutched in his muscle-riddled arms, and wrapped in what looked to be butcher's paper, was Phil. Somehow, Phil had survived the marble attack, and now, the disgusting cockroach had two of its legs in casts propped up on Hambone's bicep.

Hambone opened the door and stepped into the class-room. Miss Mobley's frantic scribbling on the chalkboard ceased and a dead silence followed. Then, to my utter horror, Hambone spoke, "I'm looking for Hashbrown."

Oh, that's not good. I thought, rounding on my heels, and nearly plowing over a wide-eyed Pigeon Criggle, who had obediently returned with Snow Cone's message.

"Pigeon, what are you doing?" I shouted more out of shock than anger.

"Mr. Brown, I have delivered your message, sir. Mr. Cone has responded with this." Pigeon dropped his glowing white head between his shoulders for emphasis. "Mr. Cone says, 'Jimmy cracked corn and he don't care' . . . whatever that means, sir." He grinned ear to ear.

"Great. That doesn't help me much now, does it, Snow?" I said to myself.

Stumped again, Pigeon looked behind him and then looked back at me with a strange look in his eye. "Um, Mr. Brown . . . I'm Pigeon," Pigeon said.

"Huh?" I asked, swinging my backpack. "Oh, I was talking to myself, Pigeon. Besides, I know Hambone's on his way. I just saw him, and he's got Phil with him to boot." I brushed passed Pigeon and dashed down the hallway. It was doubtful I would be able to survive long enough to make my appointment with Cordovo Figanewty—not with Hambone and Phil hot on my trail. I still had fourth period social studies with Mr. Blindside and then half of fifth period music with Mrs. Stone. That was too long to wait. It was clear Hambone was on the hunt, and in this school you didn't need a bloodhound to find somebody. You just needed to be either the biggest or the scariest kid in school. It just so happened that Hambone was both.

Chapter 8
Purple Duck Floaters

The sound of thunder rang out through the school. Hambone was on the move. I darted through the hallways and then on into the third-grade wing hoping to lose him. I actually caught a glimpse of the Oracle trying to poke an unsuspecting second grader with his bony finger as I bustled past.

Plastered on several of the lockers and above the drinking fountains were wanted posters, with crayon-sketched drawings of my face. Hambone wasn't offering a reward, probably because he had trouble writing numbers. I halted by one of the posters to get a closer look. What was he trying to draw? It looked as though Hambone had attempted to provide a visual aid for his posters: a plate of sunny-side eggs, bacon, and, you got it, hash browns. "Oh, that's cute."

From beyond the next hallway came the sound of heavy breathing. If I hadn't known who was tailing me, I would've thought it was a buffalo. There was no way I was going to fourth period. I would be a sitting duck in social studies.

Mr. Blindside liked to hand out ridiculous reading assignments and then take long naps at the back of the class. Hambone could easily storm the classroom to attack without any fear of the teacher waking up. Heck, even an army of trombone-playing tap dancers could have done so with the same results.

It was risky, but I knew where I needed to hide. I dropped to the floor and rummaged in my backpack for the survival kit. Grabbing what I needed, I headed for the girls' restrooms near the lunchroom and ducked quietly into the first stall. Here I should be safe for at least thirty minutes.

Usually, after four cups of hot espresso, Ms. Borfish could be seen vacating the girl's restrooms right after third period, thus rendering it a quarantine zone for the rest of the morning.

Luckily, I had my survival kit. I strapped on the gas mask and plopped down on the commode in the first stall. I needed to think. No, I needed Snow Cone, but I doubted even Pigeon would brave the death fumes of Ms. Borfish's aftermath.

Checking my watch, I noted that in exactly seventy-two minutes I would be addressing Mr. Cordovo Figanewty. If I didn't sound convincing, I might end up in a world of hurt.

What would Hambone do to me? Oh, the possibilities were endless. I quickly recalled every unfortunate injury Hambone had inflicted on his classmates in recent memory.

Humus Laredo once mistakenly sat down in Hambone's chair. The result: Humus's hips were hot-glued together. Figure that one out.

Lips Warshowski once sneezed in the back of Mr. Dittan's class and, through some freak of nature, a boogey actually traveled across the classroom and landed on Hambone's shoelace. Hambone had stretched Warshowski's lips out like banjo strings. Now Lips is always blowing kisses.

Angus "Beef" Pittman accidentally sprayed Hambone's jeans with the trick drinking fountain outside of the cafeteria.

Even Houdini would be hard pressed to find an escape route out of that trash receptacle.

And who could forget poor old Blue Dart Bowman?

All of those were minor offenses. As far as I could remember, Hambone had never actually murdered anyone. But to severely injure his cockroach. . . ? I could only imagine the retribution.

"You bone head," I moaned.

I breathed deeply through the gas mask and listened. The hallways were quiet. Was Hambone still out there? Someone pulled the bathroom door opened and yelped. "Oh, Borfish!" It was the janitor, accidentally going into the wrong restroom. From his reaction, it was clear this wasn't the first time he'd made the mistake. Mr. Hackerfist choked loudly and ran away from the bathroom shouting words like "toxic" and "fumes of doom."

I chuckled. It paid to know your way around Pordunce. I pulled the bull basher from my pocket and examined it through the protective lenses of the gas mask. It was a magnificent treasure, but would it be enough? Could I convince Mr. Figanewty the marble was valuable? I knew I needed my best performance—one worthy of the drama club.

Again the bathroom door burst open, and someone entered, hacking and spitting wildly. I cautiously opened the stall door just as Snow Cone crawled into view. He was in bad shape. Lime green in color.

Snow coughed. "Hashbrown," he said, reaching for my shirtsleeves.

"What is it, Snow? What are you doing here unprotected? This gas will take years off your life." I helped Snow Cone to his feet.

"It doesn't matter, Hash. We've got more serious problems."

"More serious than Ms. Borfish? I'm not sure I know of anything more serious than that."

"It's Whiz."

I frowned. "What about Whiz? If he needs to go that badly, there are other stalls here he can use."

"No, it's not that." Snow Cone was going limp. He had about forty-five seconds of consciousness left before the deadly gas kicked in. "Hambone has taken Whiz hostage. He strapped his arms with purple duck floaters and stuck him down into the school's main water supply. He's sent out a message."

I wobbled, nearly fainting. Now we had a hostage crisis, but why the school's water supply? It didn't make sense. "What's the message, Snow? Tell me quickly before you pass out."

"Hambone says you need to surrender or he'll never let Whiz out. Oh Hash, it's awful. He's forced Whiz to drink gallons of water. There's so much water," Snow sobbed.

Oh no! It had just dawned on me. Water and Whiz didn't mix. It was the same as fire and ice or Ms. Borfish and bran cereal. "What do I do? Tell me!"

It was too late. Snow was out cold. He curled up like a baby and sucked his thumb, dreaming no doubt of his first encounter with the Snow Cone delivery truck.

I could wait no longer. Not with Whiz, a ticking time bomb, floating around in the school's water supply. This type of emergency justified an early appointment with Cordovo Figanewty.

Heck, he drank the school's water, didn't he? Probably not, but surely someone on his staff did. And if that were true, how could he bear having a team of pee-breathing thugs hanging around.

I clutched my bull basher in my hands and dragged my

best friend out of the danger zone, propping him up against the trophy case.

"Don't worry, Snow, I'll come back for you. That's a promise." I pressed a wad of silly putty in Snow Cone's hand. I'm not exactly sure why.

I headed down the hallway straight toward the teacher's lounge. I had a date with destiny, and I wore a gas mask to prove it.

Chapter 9
Sandwiched

I was on my way into the lair of Cordovo Figanewty. Over my four plus years of attendance, I had explored almost every possible inch of Pordunce Elementary School.

Whenever Mrs. Needles, the school nurse, had an itching to check for cooties or hand out unwanted flu shots, everyone followed me to the hidden hideout beneath the boiler room. And when Luinda Sharpie went nuts one day and started practicing wrestling moves on every student in the hallways, it was I who knew which snack combination on the vending machines opened the secret passage into the gymnasium. But this was the first time I had ever dared to approach the teacher's lounge. I felt uneasy. This was uncharted territory.

The wooden door of the teacher's lounge was peppered with bullet holes. Ok, they weren't exactly bullet holes. It's a little known fact that termites plague half the school, but the pockmarked scars on the door added to the effect. I took a deep breath and knocked sharply. A rectangular slot halfway up the door opened, and a pair of sinister eyes appeared, staring down.

"Who dares disturb the domain of Mr. Figanewty?" It

was Paul Rumspill, aka The Sheik, aka The Pied Piper of Pordunce, speaking in a thick New Jersey accent, despite having been born and raised in Tacoma, Washington.

"I . . . uh . . . have . . . um . . . an appointment with Cordovo Figanewty," I said in a high-pitched chirp, sounding more or less like the chime of a microwave stuffed with a steaming plate of hash brown casserole.

"That's Mr. Figanewty to you," The Sheik said. "Who is you, anyways?"

"My name's Hashbrown."

"What was that? Speak up louder, or I'll pound you one." It was common knowledge that The Sheik was hard of hearing. Why Cordovo Figanewty had chosen him to be the doorman of his lair confused me, seeing as how The Sheik made everyone repeat themselves over and over again.

"My name's Hashbrown Winters, sir. I have an appointment at—"

"That's enough outta yous. I heard yous the first time."

Oh yeah, just a little tidbit of important information. The various members of the Figanewty Organization had a tendency to use the words "yous guys" a lot. (Not to be mistaken with the group Ewe's Guys, best known for their smash hit Baaad Boys.) It took a little getting used to.

"Hashbrown, you say? Stand right there while I consult my ledger." The Sheik disappeared from the slot, and I could hear the sound of rifling pages. His uni-browed eyes returned. "Yeah, Hashbrown. It says here you have an appointment with Mr. Figanewty at 11:45. You are forty-five minutes early. Come back later." The slot almost closed.

I shot my fingers up to stop the slot from closing. "No, wait! It's an emergency!"

The Sheik's eyes peered down. "Excuse you? What did you just say? I don't waits for nobody."

"I understand, sir, but if I don't speak with Mr. Figanewty right now this whole school is in a lot of trouble."

The Sheik chuckled. "Whatever, kid. We don't reschedule for nobody. Come back later."

I panicked but managed to calm myself. You had to stay calm when dealing with dangerous people like the Figanewty Organization. "All right, I suppose I can wait for my appointment, but I doubt that'll matter much."

"That's more like it. Now scram, kid." The Sheik was about to end the conversation completely, but I fired back.

"I suppose you'll be the one that has to explain to Mr. Figanewty why his slushy tastes like pee. I, myself, would hate to have that responsibility. Especially when Cordovo finds out it's your fault the whole school's water supply has been contaminated." There was a brief silence in which I was certain I could hear the calm warbling of geese bathing in the pond outside. Then the silence was immediately replaced with the piercing sound of The Sheik hissing like a spent tea kettle.

"What did you say?" he asked, his eyes narrowing.

Normally, I'm not bothered by someone narrowing their eyes. My mother does it all the time, as do most of my teachers. It really isn't that big of a deal. Why do they narrow their eyes? It seems silly to me. Do they actually think they can see farther with their eyes narrowed?

Do you want to know what I see when I narrow my eyes? The back of my eyelids. I just simply ignore people when they choose to do it. However, when someone as fierce and horrifying as The Sheik narrows his eyes at you, it'd be wise to at least act terrified. In truth, if you had happened to be traveling down that particular hallway at the precise moment that The Sheik narrowed his eyes at me, you would have seen the faint glow of lasers shooting out of his eyeballs as they danced across my face like barbarian fireflies.

Figuring I was about to die anyway, and that being pummeled by The Sheik was probably more merciful than anything Hambone could do, I spoke on with confidence.

"With all due respect, Mr. The Sheik, I think you and I both know what I have to say to Mr. Figanewty is probably more important than trying to stick to schedule. We are in state of red alert, and I have something worth Mr. Figanewty's time."

The result was amazing. The Sheik's eyes came back to their original form. His eyebrows actually raised slightly in thought. "Don't you move a muscle," he ordered. Then he disappeared.

The next moments lurched along slower than a club-footed sloth. Fortunately, the hall remained quiet, allowing me time to mull over my next plan of attack. If The Sheik came back and told me I was out of luck, I was fully prepared to do the unthinkable. That's right—fall on the floor and cry like a two-year-old.

The door creaked open, and rich Italian music wafted out of the teacher's lounge. The Sheik grabbed me by the scruff of my neck and propelled me into the room. It was at that moment I realized where I actually stood. Sitting at the table, twiddling all manner of weaponry in their hands were five frightening members of Cordovo Figanewty's organization. I actually made eye contact with Razor Cannelloni and Squid Madsen, both of whom were responsible for the December Doorbell Ditching Fiasco. That's right, the one you probably read about in all the papers. Of course, no one could prove it was them.

Tony Ten Fingers pushed away from the table and stared me down. I instinctively looked at Tony's fingers. They were still all there. *Amazing*, I thought.

"What are you staring at, kid?" Tony asked, popping his knuckles. It sounded like ten cannons had just gone off.

"Uh . . . fwa-ha dooga," I answered. I actually hoped to say something along the lines of "Nothing man, what's up with you." You know, sound like I was cool and that standing in front of Tony Ten Fingers was just something I did for fun. Instead I came off sounding like I was ready to hurl into the trash can or better yet, pull a Whiz Peterson on the floor.

"What did you call me?" Tony asked, scratching his head.

I got control of myself. "Oh, nothing, just—"

"Mr. Figanewty will see you now, and he's not happy 'bout it," The Sheik chimed in, saving me from any further embarrassment. "Tommy and Petey will walk you in." The Sheik motioned toward the other two sitting at the table, who immediately rose and crowded me in at either side.

Tommy Pastrami and Petey Provolone, the sandwich twins, were almost identical in appearance and towered over my head. They got their names for two reasons. One, they didn't eat anything but sandwiches. It didn't matter if it was cold cuts or a hot meatball. They enjoyed every kind of lunch meat, even olive loaf. Yep, they were the real deal. The second reason for their nickname was that no one entered into Cordovo's office unless he was sandwiched between the two of them.

I had been warned about the sandwich twins' body odor, and I quickly held my breath, but not before catching a whiff. It was a mixture of Dijon mustard, dill pickles, and honey-baked ham.

"You may be my half-cousin's little friend, but if I hear one word that you've wasted Mr. Figanewty's time," Tony warned, watching the sandwich twins escort me out of the room. I swallowed hard. Tony was certainly a bowlful of kittens.

The sandwich twins lead me through a maze of ready-to-assemble furniture boxes, freshly dry-cleaned suits, and towering bags stuffed with green bills. It was amazing how big the teacher's lounge actually was. All this time, we were lead to believe the teachers were mistreated with hardly any room at all to relax. Well, that was true now, ever since the Figanewty family moved in, forcing the teaching staff to relocate to the sixth-grade wing's janitorial closet.

Finally, after endless walking, we approached a walnut door with stained-glass decorations. The door opened and I saw Vice Principal Humidor shaking Cordovo's hand.

"Thank you, Mr. Figanewty, you are most gracious," Vice Principal Humidor said as he exited the office, staring down at me as he passed. "Excuse me, Mr. Winters, I don't think you've got a pass to be out of class right now, do you?"

What was I to do now? In the next millisecond I pieced together a believable excuse. "I . . . um . . . was going to sell raffle tickets for the talent show."

Vice Principal Humidor smiled. "I'll forget I saw you here, if you forget seeing me. Deal?"

I nodded. Of course, in my mind I recorded every detail of the scene. This would make quite a lunchroom story, if I ever lived to tell it.

"Go in, chump," Tommy grunted. I tiptoed forward and smiled pathetically. Cordovo did not return the smile. Instead he gave me a dark scowl.

The don of Pordunce Elementary wasn't actually, what I'd expected. This was the first time I'd ever seen Cordovo up close. From this view, I received a very clear image. Cordovo Figanewty's skin was pale and flaky. His hair was sleek black and receding badly. His nose was pudgy and pinched, and his cheeks puffed out like a gold fish.

Despite his appearance, there was an air of importance surrounding him. He was powerful, no doubt about that. In front of him were a beautifully sliced steak and a glass of melon juice.

"Don't waste Mr. Figanewty's time," Petey Provolone hissed. "Speak up."

I gulped. This was it. My moment of truth. If ever I needed heavenly wisdom, now was the time. "I . . . Hashbrown."

WHAT?! I, Hashbrown? What was that garbage?

Clearly everyone else in the room was thinking the same thing. In only a few seconds, I had already managed to sound like an idiot.

Shaking my head, I tried again. "What I mean is, I have something very important to tell you, and I'd like to buy your protection."

Cordovo Figanewty looked thoughtfully for a moment and then made a waving gesture with his hand, signaling it was okay for me to continue.

"Go on, but be quick about it," Tommy said.

"Right. As you probably all know Hambone Oxcart is a menace to society," I said, nodding for emphasis.

Cordovo mumbled something I couldn't understand.

"Mr. Figanewty says he's sorry, but he has no idea who you're talking about," Tommy said.

"What? You've got to be joking me!" I exclaimed, but immediately wished I hadn't. That was way too disrespectful. Instead of getting angry, Cordovo smiled and mumbled something else. Again, I couldn't understand and looked to Tommy for an explanation.

"Mr. Figanewty says he doesn't joke. Who are we talking about here?"

"Hambone Oxcart. The man-child. The fence-eater. The kid with the pet cockroach for crying out loud."

Mr. Figanewty chuckled.

"Mr. Figanewty says he recalls seeing someone with a rather larger cockroach in the hallways. He finds him very humorous."

Imagine having been dropped into the middle of a scary mafia movie where everyone speaks with thick New Jersey accents. So thick you'd be better off reading subtitles. Yeah, that was how it was in the teacher's lounge at Pordunce Elementary.

"Mr. Figanewty, Hambone's not humorous. He's not funny at all. He's awful and he wants to fold me up, wrap me in aluminum foil, and cram me into his lunch box."

"Wait a minute?" Petey piped in. "I think I heard about this. You mean to tell me you're the guy that tried to snuff out his cockroach?"

"That was an accident," I said, shaking my head. "The freaky thing talked to me. It tried to attack me."

Petey began to laugh. "Yo, this guy's the one everyone's gabbin' about. He's a real ringer, this one."

Mr. Figanewty frowned and mumbled.

"Oh, sorry, sir. I won't speak out of turn again," Petey apologized.

Cordovo Figanewty sighed with disappointment, but then looked at me with interest. He swallowed what must have been an enormous piece of steak and spoke clearly for the first time. "Go ahead. What are you asking for?"

"Mr. Figanewty says for you to go ahead. He says—" Tommy started.

"You moron. I have finished chewing my meal. You no longer need to interpret for me," Cordovo said. Tommy lowered his head in embarrassment.

Frank L. Cole

"Well . . . uh . . ." I started. I was getting a little confused but remembered quickly. "Sir, I need protection and I need help for one of my friends, Whiz Peterson."

"Oh, the pant-wetter?" Cordovo asked.

"Yeah, you know him?" I answered.

"I know him," Cordovo said, shaking his head in what looked to be disappointment.

"That can't be good."

"No, it's not good. That boy has a bladder the size of an acorn."

"I know. It's a modern medical mystery." I made a mental note to tell Whiz he may have made it on Cordovo Figanewty's hit list. That would be a whole other problem to worry about. "So I'm guessing you've heard what's happened with the school's water supply?" I asked.

"We've heard," Mr. Figanewty said, glancing at his fingernails. "But it's not our concern."

"What if I made it worth your while to make it your concern?"

"I suppose you have brought sufficient payment for a request such as this."

Here it goes. If only I had a drum roll. I needed to create the illusion that what I was about to take out of my pocket was more valuable than gold. I began my theatrics by looking over both of my shoulders to make sure no one else was watching. This worked. All three of the mob members became curious about what I was doing. Next, I let out a loud sigh, similar to the sound a steam locomotive makes when it applies its breaks. I wanted to make it seem like it took all of my strength to part with the marble. The sandwich twins were actually crouched down low in curiosity, and Cordovo rose to his feet hoping for a better look.

"Now, believe me when I tell you this was not easy to

come by," I whispered. "I doubt there are more than three of these in existence. This is something so rare and so valuable, I can't believe I'm actually going to offer it." They were buying it, every last, lying word I spat out. I had managed to convince the three of them I had brought Mr. Figanewty something more than worthwhile.

Feeling good about the act, I pulled the bull basher from my pocket and held it up to the light. As if on cue, a beam of light passed through the marble like it was a biblical artifact. The result was priceless; Cordovo Figanewty, Tommy Pastrami, and Petey Provolone expelled a long, loud "Oooooooh!"

"Yeah, believe me, its real," I said. I handed the marble carefully to Tommy's eager fingers. Tommy held it close to his eye and examined it with the use of a tiny magnifying glass.

"Oh my, Mr. Figanewty, this is nice, real nice. Solid glass, unbelievable color and clarity. I'd say . . . what? Two . . . two and a half karats?" Tommy asked.

"Three," I answered. I had no clue what a karat was.

Petey slapped his hip. "Three karats? No way!"

"Yes way," I said. I must've looked like a goof ball the way I smiled so big, but I couldn't help myself. Cordovo Figanewty was honestly impressed with my marble. There's no way he was going to turn it away.

Just then, Tony Ten Fingers entered the room. "Mr. Figanewty, we have a situation."

All four of us looked up from our marble-gawking. "Yes, what is it, Tony?" Cordovo asked.

Tony tossed a scrap of paper onto the desk. It was one of Hambone's wanted posters from the hallways. I felt my stomach churn. We leaned in close as Mr. Figanewty held up the note for all to read.

Hambone had scribbled again in crayon, across his drawing. His message, though severely misspelled, was clear:

I want no truble with u. Just sind out the Tot

"Send out the tot?" I asked. "What's he talking about?"

"I think he means you, tater tot," Cordovo said, turning the message over in his hand.

"Ah, poop," I said.

"Where's this Hambone at right now?" Cordovo asked.

"He's pulled the principal's bench out into the hallway and is sitting across from the lounge. He's also holding some sort of insect in his hands. I'm not sure why. Maybe he's trying to send a message."

"That would be Phil," I said, smacking my head with my hand so hard I felt my brain rattle around like a marble.

"Should I deal with him?" Tony asked, folding his arms menacingly.

"Not in front of the lounge," Cordovo said. "I don't want to draw any unnecessary attention to our hideout." Mr. Figanewty looked out the window, deep in thought.

"Then should I give up the tot?"

Cordovo didn't answer, which freaked me out just a little bit.

I cleared my throat. "I think that would be a bad idea," I squeaked.

Tony glared down at me. "A bad idea, eh? Seems to me, you brought this trouble to our doorstep. I say if this Hambone character wants the little guy, we give him the little guy."

I looked pleadingly at Cordovo, who had yet to look away from the window. "What about my marble?" I asked.

"What about your *what*?" Tony asked. "Have you been eatin' rotten oatmeal kid?"

Finally, Cordovo returned his attention to the bull basher. The strange looking sixth grader now held my life in his hands. What would he do? Would he turn me over to the hippo-human hybrid, or would he take the marble as payment?

I had to seal the deal. I'm sure my voice sounded like that of a constipated guinea pig but I didn't care. "Think about it, Mr. Figanewty," I said. "That marble is all yours in exchange for a teeny, tiny thing; just protection against Hambone, the death dealer of Pordunce, and rescuing my pal Whiz before he piddles in the water system." Everyone in the room stared at Cordovo Figanewty. "What do you say? Do we have a deal?"

If for some reason, he decided it wasn't worth it, then all of my troubles would be for naught. I felt a pit form in my stomach as I waited. Mr. Figanewty placed the marble on his desk and rolled it around with his fingers. Looking toward the ceiling, he became lost in deep concentration. I prepared myself to tumble to the ground and beg. Then, with a slight wave of his hand, the meeting was over. I didn't even scream when Cordovo pressed the red button on his desk that opened the trap door beneath my chair.

Down I fell, like I was tumbling around in a giant toilet without water. Of course, I hated to think what that made me. When I looked up as Cordovo's office swept from my view, I saw Mr. Figanewty slicing a large piece off his steak and jabbing it in his mouth. The marble was still on the table.

"Does that mean we have a deal?" I yelled. But then I

was alone, swirling around and around, wondering if that slide of doom would ever end. Finally, I landed in a heap of garbage behind the school.

I stood up and brushed banana peels and used tissues from off my shirt. "Man, I've got to put one of those in my tree house," I said, pulling a Q-tip out from beneath my shirt collar.

Chapter 10
Whiz's Tale

It took me five minutes to navigate my way through a few of my secret routes so that I could get back into the hallways undetected. I wondered if Hambone still sat on the principal's bench outside of the teacher's lounge. Plus, I wasn't exactly positive Mr. Figanewty would help me. *What if he just took the marble for the heck of it?* What if I was still on my own?

I glanced down at my watch and noted the time was nearing noon. In less than two hours there would be a show-down on the playground, and it would be so much more fun if I had Tony Ten Fingers on my side. As I rounded the corner, I tripped over Snow Cone who was beginning to revive.

"Hashbrown!" Snow Cone exclaimed, pulling himself up and nearly collapsing.

"Easy, pal. The effects of the gas take a while to wear off. You should find some place to rest." I looked down the hall for a bench we could sit on.

"I'll be fine, Hash. Why was I looking for you? I can't remember."

"Memory loss. You and Measles are going to have more

in common than the rest of us." Poor Snow Cone. Who could ask for a better friend?

Ms. Borfish burst through the cafeteria doors, beelining for the forbidden restroom. "Shouldn't have had that seventh cup!" she hollered, hurdling over the top of Snow Cone. She was surprisingly nimble for a lunch lady.

"I guess we made it out of there just in time, huh?" I said.

"Wait a minute." Snow jerked up. "I remember now. What time is it?"

I read my watch. "11:55."

Snow Cone moaned. "You dummy, you're ten minutes late for your appointment."

The sound of Ms. Borfish's lovely singing voice echoed through the hallway. We both grimaced.

"Oh, I already went," I said, sticking my hand under Snow Cone's arm and helping him to his feet.

"What?" Snow asked.

"Yeah, I just left good ol' Mr. Figanewty's office a few minutes ago."

"And you're still alive? Wait a minute, I didn't survive the gas, did I?" Snow darted his head in either direction. "And heaven looks like elementary school."

"Trust me, we're both very much alive, at least for now."

"How did it go?" Snow asked.

"I don't know, Snow. One minute I'm showing off my prized bull basher, and Mr. Figanewty is loving every bit of it. The next minute, Hambone's outside the office calling me out, and I'm blasting down a garbage chute."

"You've got to be kidding me," Snow gasped. "Did he take the marble then?"

"He took it all right." I pulled out my pockets to show they were empty.

"That's got to mean something good, doesn't it?"

"I hope so. It was a bull basher, one of a kind. I know they saw the value in it, but I have no way of knowing for sure." I ran my fingers through my hair. "Come on, let's get to lunch. I have a feeling Ms. Borfish is about to send this hallway into uncharted territories if you know what I'm saying. Besides, I want to be front and center when the news spreads."

And spread it did. By 12:05 everyone with a pulse knew about my meeting with Cordovo Figanewty. The lunchroom buzzed with excitement. What would happen to me? What would happen to Hambone? What would the organization do to him?

Something fluttered up to my side and tugged at my shirtsleeve. I instinctively jumped but relaxed when I saw it was only Pigeon.

"Mr. Brown, I'm so happy to see you still breathing. Is there anything I can do for you? Any messages you would like sent?"

I laughed. "Sure, Pigeon, go tell me mom to wash and press my church suit. I want to like nice for my funeral." I said, trying to make light of the situation.

"Why certainly, sir," Pigeon said. Before I had a chance to snatch him by his arm, Pigeon screeched out of the lunchroom, a bird on a mission.

"That will go over great with my mom."

"Come on, Hash," Snow Cone said. "Don't be in such a bad mood."

I would've answered my pal, but just then a commotion rose in the lunch room as students spotted Whiz Peterson entering from the hallway.

He had been released.

But that would mean. . . . I about fell over. I watched

in awe as a very confused and soaking wet Whiz zigzagged through the rows of students and made his way toward our usual lunch table.

If Whiz was no longer floating around in the school's water supply, then somebody must have got him out. The only somebody brave enough to go up against Hambone Oxcart was someone from the Figanewty Organization. Cordovo had wasted no time delivering on his end of the bargain.

I beamed from ear to ear. Nothing could ruin my mood. Even when Ms. Borfish grinned and plopped down two extra helpings of hash browns on my plate, I merely smiled and said, "Thank you, Ms. Borfish. Is that a new hair net? It's certainly nice. It brings out the color of your mole."

I sat down at the center of the lunch table, and the rest of the club cheered, holding their cartons of chocolate milk up high.

"Hear, hear! Hooray for Hashbrown!" Four Hips exclaimed, pausing briefly from his slop to salute. "To the greatest guy a kid could know. Are you going to eat all of your lunch? I'm almost finished with mine."

"You know, Four Hips, I think I'm in the mood for my lunch today. I'm not sure why," I said as I scooped up a heaping forkful of hash browns and jabbed them in my mouth. They had never tasted so good. We all looked at Whiz, waiting for him to tell his wonderful story.

"I'd have come here sooner, but I drank too much water. Oh and by the way, the bathrooms in the east hall are pretty much out of order. No need to ask me why," Whiz said, yawning. "Boy, am I tired."

Measles' feet drummed excitedly against the lunchroom floor. "So what happened?" he asked. "How did they do it?"

"How did who do what?" Whiz asked. He grabbed a hard-crusted roll from Bubblegum Bulkins' plate and nibbled on it indifferently.

"How did Mr. Figanewty save you from Hambone's clutches?" Bubblegum Bulkins asked.

Whiz chewed and a look of amazement formed on his face. "That was who that was? I didn't think he was that tall."

"Nah, it couldn't have been Cordovo Figanewty. He wouldn't do a job like that on his own," said Snow Cone. "My guess is it was Tony Ten Fingers that saved you."

"Tony Ten Fingers!" Whiz shouted and then groaned. "Oh man, I thought I emptied it all." You guessed it, Whiz had whizzed. The rest of the group slid a few feet away. "It's all a blur. I don't remember much. One moment I'm minding my own business, just buying pencils from Luinda at the school store. Oh and by the way, did you know she can chew a pencil eraser into paste? It's quite impressive." Everyone nodded. "Oh and Snow, she's got it for you bad."

Snow dropped his head on his folded arms as everyone laughed. "Don't remind me, Whiz," Snow said.

"Yeah, she was wearing a T-shirt that said 'LS and SCJ together forever' with a big heart made out of puff paint. I think she made it herself," Whiz added. "Anyway, there I stood, like I said, minding my own business, when all of a sudden everything went black. Next thing I know, I'm bobbing up and down like a buoy in this big ol' tank of water. Hambone stood above me laughing and he had Phil with him as well. I thought you said Phil went splat, Hashbrown?"

"I know. I thought he *did*," I said.

"Well, he wasn't a splat, that's for sure," Whiz continued. "It was the creepiest thing I've ever seen. Phil wore a cast on two of his legs and a beret on his head."

"A beret?" Four Hips chimed in. "I never knew he was French."

"When Hambone closed the lid on the water tank, I thought I was a goner. Then, I think I may have dozed off. It was very relaxing you know, floating in all that water with floaties on your arms. Suddenly, just about twenty minutes ago, the lid opened, and there was this giant guy standing above me."

"Tony Ten Fingers!" Measles said.

Whiz piddled again.

"Stop saying that!" he shouted. "Yeah, he pulled me up and said something like 'If you know what's good for yous, you'll hold it until I get you outta there.' A quick pit stop at the restrooms, and here I am. It's all very bizarre."

"Whiz, I'm sorry you had to go through all of that just for me," I said.

Whiz smiled. "Hey, what are friends for? Besides, I got to swim through Mr. Fidgewarbles' entire lecture in my own private swimming pool. You can't beat that."

"Speaking of which, you *were* able to hold it while you were in there, weren't you, Whiz?" Snow Cone asked. Everyone else fell silent in anticipation.

"Why," Whiz answered, "was I supposed to?" Snow Cone and I exchanged looks of horror, just as Whiz began to laugh. "Oh, man. You should've seen your faces. Of course, I held it. I drink that water too, you dips."

"Hashbrown do you know what this means?" Four Hips asked. "You did it. You made the hallways safe for all of us. There's no way Hambone will mess with any of us from now on. Not with the Figanewty family on our side."

I hadn't thought about it that way. Was it possible that I, Hashbrown Winters, had not only saved my own skin, but also done a great service for all of my classmates at Pordunce

Elementary? "I guess you're right, Four Hips. I don't suppose we'll hear much from Hambone after today."

The table erupted with cheers. I sat back feeling triumphant, smiling, and soaking it all in.

Chapter 11

Showdown by the Oak Tree

Recess.

2:30 pm.

The playground.

It was where everything important to a student at Pordunce Elementary happened. It was where the real education took place. Boys were made into men; romances were ignited and snuffed out just as quickly in a whirlwind of spitballs and dirt clods. Nicknames were earned and taken away. Over the past four and a half years, I had spent two hundred and seventy hours of my life on that playground. As I mentioned before, there wasn't much to do on the actual playground attractions, but it was what happened at the marble pit and just beyond the swing sets that mattered.

On this particular afternoon, an uncommon breeze blew through the trees, foreshadowing that something was about to happen on that hallowed ground that would change my life forever. You could feel the electricity.

I stepped off the sidewalk and onto the playground. Despite having the knowledge Cordovo Figanewty had my back, my nerves were shot. First graders, who, even at their tender age, had already felt the brunt of Hambone's ways, pitched roses at my feet. Everything rode on this afternoon.

At the edge of the teeter-totters there stood an old oak tree. It was the symbol of the playground and had been there longer than the school itself. It was also the home of three very irate, rabid squirrels, but that's another subject altogether.

At the base of the tree standing like a gunslinger in a showdown was Hambone. He wore his usual stained T-shirt and ripped jeans, but now added a new piece of clothing—a red windbreaker with the sleeves tied around his neck. In the blowing wind it looked more like a cape then anything else.

I felt a shiver travel up my spine, and I slowed down for a moment. I was about to face the arch villain of Pordunce Elementary, one of the elite bad guys.

"You ready for this?" Snow Cone asked as he joined me by my side.

"What are you doing here, Snow?" I asked, jumping back in surprise. "I have to do this alone. I don't want anyone else to get hurt."

"Yeah, yeah," Measles said, appearing to my right. "The way I figure it, maybe Hambone hasn't caught the spots yet. My condition could come in handy."

"Guys, seriously," I said, but before I could continue, Bubblegum, Four Hips, and Whiz fell in line next to me. The smell of watermelon bubble gum filled my nostrils; Bulkins was taking this seriously. Whiz wore rubber pants, and Four Hips shoveled a two-foot long churro smothered in cream cheese down his throat.

"We're all here, Hash, whether you like it or not," Snow said.

"You could turn back now, if you wanted," I said with a grin.

"None of us wants to," Whiz answered.

"Speak for yourself," Four Hips said, wiping cream cheese from his lips.

It was good to have all of my friends next to me. Out of the corner of my eye, I saw something that boosted my confidence even more. There was Cordovo Figanewty along with Tony Ten Fingers rounding the merry-go-round. From that distance, they looked like ordinary elementary school children, but I knew it was only an illusion. I began to walk down the hill toward the tree with briskness in my step.

"So you're sure, they'll go through with it?" Snow Cone asked.

"Nope, but what can I do now?"

In just a matter of moments, we passed the clump box, the balance beam, the flower garden where Ms. Pinkens had planted an army of Venus Fly traps, and the jungle gym. All the while, students from every walk of life and every grade swarmed around me like curious bees. Several second graders began to chant, "Dead man walking," as I passed. I ignored this as best I could.

I hesitated. Misty Piccolo stood by the swing sets just on the outskirts of where the showdown would happen. I had completely forgotten she'd be there. Would she rush to my side when Hambone had done his worst?

Finally, we reached the roots of the old oak tree and Hambone.

Hambone glowered. "You're very brave, Hashbrown, but you must be very stupid," he said, holding the injured Phil in his arms.

"Oh, I don't know, Hambone, I'm feeling pretty lucky today," I replied, my voice trembling with excitement as I looked around at my group of friends. "I think you've done enough bullying around here, and it's time you moved along." There was a rumble of voices as several students in the crowd agreed with me. Of course, as soon as Hambone made eye contact with any of them, they pretended to whistle and looked the other way.

"I don't think so. This is my school. No one can hurt my Phil and get away with it." Hambone growled.

"It was an accident, Hambone. Besides, Phil attacked me first. I was just defending myself."

Phil hissed.

"It doesn't matter now. In a day or two, no one will remember who you were." With that said, Hambone took a thundering step toward me with his hands clinched into fists.

"Not so fast, Hambone." It was Cordovo Figanewty. He had taken his time crossing the playground, but managed to arrive at the oak tree at the right moment. "You're not going to do anything to Hashbrown. He's a personal friend of mine, and I wouldn't like to see him hurt."

"This has nothing to do with you, sir," Hambone said with respect. It was the first time he had ever used the word "sir." There was a gasp in the crowd, and several students actually fainted.

"Oh, I believe it does," Cordovo said, nodding at me. "I made it my business. Now move along before this gets ugly."

"You heard Mr. Figanewty," Tony Ten Fingers said, popping his knuckles.

Hambone paused. He appeared to be actually thinking things through. Maybe he would walk away. Maybe he would leave without resorting to violence. I had never truly realized how much power Cordovo Figanewty possessed. As far as I was concerned, Cordovo was the most powerful person on the earth.

"Do me a favor, Hambone," Cordovo continued. "Walk away and never bother these kids again."

As dumb as Hambone was, he wasn't about to cross Cordovo Figanewty, especially while Tony Ten Fingers stood at his side. After several nail-biting moments, Hambone began to turn around. I grew excited and almost cheered for joy. Almost.

A blaring police car with flashing blue and red lights screeched onto the playground and came to a halt just inches away from the scene. Every student gaped as two men dressed in black suits, wearing sunglasses and flashing their badges, burst out of the car. Everyone froze, including Hambone. The men walked quickly up to Cordovo and Tony Ten Fingers.

"Cordovo Figanewty?" one of the officers asked.

"That's Mr. Figanewty to you," Tony Ten Fingers blurted out.

"Pipe down, kid," the other officer ordered and to everyone's amazement, Tony obeyed.

"Are you Cordovo Figanewty?" the first officer asked again.

"Maybe I am, maybe I'm not. Who wants to know?" Cordovo asked with an air of confidence.

"Sorry, kid, but your daddy's in some trouble, and you need to go now."

Cordovo chuckled. "My daddy?"

"Yes, Mr. Agnacio Figanewty has made a deal with the feds and is entering the witness relocation program. It appears all of your family's funding has been cut off and you will be moving immediately."

"What?" Cordovo Figanewty asked as tears bubbled up from his eyes. "Who took my daddy's money?"

Measles laughed. "He said daddy." No one else dared

laugh, and Measles played it off that he was suffering from a temporary hallucination.

"Say your good-byes to your little friends and hop in the car." The officer opened the black vehicle's door, and Cordovo Figanewty climbed into the seat with his head bowed.

"And you," the other officer pointed to Tony. "Is your name Tony Spelunker?" Tony's eyes grew wide, and he nodded. "Yeah, you too kid, say your good-byes and hop in the car."

"Why, what did my daddy do?" Tony was also almost in tears. It was very disturbing. No one standing in the audience knew what to make of the situation.

"You don't want to know, kid. Believe me, you don't want to know. Both of you will be moving very far away from here, and these kids will never see you again. You will be changing your names and probably your clothes. Let's get a move on."

It was blindingly fast. One moment they were there scaring away Hambone, the next moment they were gone, never to return to Pordunce Elementary. Later on we heard rumors that Cordovo Figanewty and Tony Ten Finger's names were changed to Terry Liverburst and Hugh Codmuffin.

I was so shocked at what had just happened, I completely forgot about Hambone and Phil. But Hambone wasn't about to be deterred again. He readied himself to charge.

"Wait just a second!" I shouted loud enough to startle the giant. I surprised myself with how forceful I sounded. Over a hundred kids had crowded beneath the old oak tree, craning their necks to try to see above the front, and dodging the onslaught of pelting acorns from the angered rabid squirrels.

Hambone snarled. "You're mine, Hashbrown. No one

else is around to save you." he said. From that close up, Hambone looked like a caveman. His sunken eyes scowled at me beneath his caterpillar eyebrows. For crying out loud, he had a five o'clock shadow, and it was only 2:40.

I needed my wits now more than ever. "That may be so, but I've got something to say before you do what you've got to do." *What to say? What to say?* My mind raced as I thought about my last words. I wanted them to be profound, special, something the students of Pordunce Elementary would remember for years to come. I wanted the name Hashbrown mentioned only with reverence. With the right words, I could be immortalized. They would erect a shrine to my memory in the school halls where children of all ages would come once a year to lay flowers and cry at my passing. There would be books written of my heroics, a broadway musical, movies, even a school holiday each year to—

"Hashbrown, say something!" Snow Cone slapped me on the back of the head and brought me back from my daydream. I must've been like that for a good two minutes. I shook away my thoughts and realized the entire school playground was silently waiting for what I was about to say. Even Hambone had not moved from his spot.

Swallowing dryly, I scanned the eyes of each of my closest pals. "Hambone, you've been the head bully of Pordunce Elementary School since the first day you stepped foot on these hallowed grounds. Every day, we students walk the halls in fear of you. You have eaten our lunches, ripped our underwear, and stolen our action figures." There was a murmur in the crowd as many students nodded in agreement. "Because of you, not one of us has had an enjoyable half an hour of recess. Because of you, over thirty first graders received unwanted nicknames." I looked into the crowd and saw Toeless Kiegan, No Knees Wiggly, and Eight Eyes

Benford glaring angrily at Hambone. "But why, Hambone? I ask why?"

"Yeah why?" Whiz shouted, but stopped himself as Hambone popped a knuckle in his finger. Whiz looked down in agony but smiled when he realized he was still wearing rubber pants. He had nothing to worry about for now.

"Why must you torture us?" I continued. "Is it because you're the biggest? The hairiest? No, I think not." Hambone looked worriedly at the gathering students. Everyone was gaining courage from my speech. I was making history at that very moment. "I think it's because you're scared."

"Scared?" Hambone asked, his voice cracking.

"Scared?" Four Hips asked, scratching his head and ramming half a caramel apple in his mouth.

"Yeah, scared," I answered. "You're scared because you know if we all stand together against you, you'll be finished. If we put our feet down and join together, you will lose. You're scared Hambone, because we're stronger than you. And now it is time for you to realize you can take our lunch money, you can pound our faces, but you will never take OUR RECESS!" I screamed at the top of my lungs, and a hundred students echoed shouts in unison. I shook from head to toe, but I had never felt so alive. Misty was in the crowd, her eyes filled with tears. I had done it. I had stood up to Hambone and won. I was a hero. A legend.

"Hashbrown! Hashbrown! Hashbrown!" the crowd chanted my name. Several spectators plucked white handkerchiefs from their backpacks and waved them wildly in the air. Snow Cone looked at me, smiling from ear to ear. They were about to hoist me up on their shoulders and parade me around the playground when a loud sound pierced the cheering.

Phil the cockroach was hissing.

Immediately, everyone fell silent. Even the acorn-throwing squirrels ceased for a moment.

Hambone started to laugh. "That was very funny, Hashbrown," he said. "For a moment you had me worried, but I just remembered one very one important thing."

I looked from Phil to Hambone. "What's that?"

"I'm not here to beat all these kids up. Just you."

With the snap of his wrist, Hambone grabbed me by my collar and pulled me into his death grip. I could only whimper. "Now I've got you," he said.

I looked pleadingly out at the crowd of students with the hope of finding anyone brave enough to save him. The crowd screamed as Hambone raised his fist into the air, preparing to strike.

The sound of Tarzan swinging through the trees erupted over the screaming as Snow Cone jumped out and clung to Hambone's arm before he could deliver his deadly blow. It was a moment of bravery, one I would never forget. Snow Cone dangled from Hambone's arm like a lugey clinging to a lamp post. He pounded his fists with all of his might against the giant bully's shoulder, but the barrage of punching had little effect. Hambone laughed as he flung Snow Cone off his arm.

"Snow!" I yelled, but the haunting sounds of Hambone's chuckles filled my ears.

"Bye, bye, Hashbrown," he growled.

Suddenly, there was Luinda Sharpie, decked out in her amateur wrestling garb and snorting like a wild bull. "Don't you ever hurt my Snow Cone!" she shouted. Cupping her hands around her lips, she released a blood-curdling scream that sounded like the voice of a wookie. It was the call of The Manatee, the sound that preceded her signature move The Manatee Maul.

Hambone had little time to react as Luinda charged at him with amazing speed. The impact uprooted his feet and actually sent him flailing through the air like a cannonball. Of course, I was unfortunately in tow, but that mattered little. Hambone somersaulted against the tree and collapsed, releasing his grip. I immediately ran to safety. No one dared say a word as all eyes rested on Luinda Sharpie. She began stomping her feet again, preparing for another charge.

Hambone looked out of it. His eyes were circling around in an utter daze. After getting to his feet, he searched the ground for Phil whom he had flung from his hand during the rampage. Phil had survived, but he was very perturbed. The cockroach lay overturned on his back. His unbroken legs were scampering wildly in place. Hambone plucked Phil up and then turned shakily toward Luinda.

"What happened?" he muttered softly.

"The Manatee happened," Luinda said in response.

Hambone blinked his eyes into focus and saw Luinda truly for the first time.

"Luinda?" he asked, rubbing the back of his head.

"That's right," The Manatee answered. Then something no one saw coming happened. Hambone blushed. His stubbly cheeks turned red and his lips pulled back in an uncomfortable grin. What was happening? No one knew. But suddenly, there was Luinda blushing and smiling back.

"Um . . ." I started, but Measles grabbed my arm.

"Don't say a word, Hashbrown," he said.

So I didn't. Instead, we all watched as something magical happened.

I had heard of this thing called love at first sight, but until that breezy afternoon on the Pordunce Elementary playground, I never believed it to be true. Hambone was love struck. To him, Luinda Sharpie was the most beautiful creature ever to grace his presence.

We all looked at each other in amazement, knowing what we were seeing. We couldn't help ourselves and burst into laughter. But Hambone and Luinda didn't even notice. What was even more amazing was the fact that Luinda returned Hambone's gaze with a equal interest. She removed her red facemask and shook the hair out of her eyes. The two behemoths clasped hands and made goo-goo eyes at each other. It was appalling. They began to make their way away from the crowd, but Luinda stopped suddenly and turned, looking sadly at Snow Cone.

"I'm sorry, Snow. I'm so sorry. We were great together, but that was another time. I have to move on, and I'm going to have to break up with you. I hope you'll understand," she said, blowing a sloppy kiss in Snow's direction.

I smirked. "Break up with you?" I asked as we watched Hambone and Luinda trudge off together. "She's one confused puppy, isn't she?"

"Yeah . . ." Snow said, dreamily. "But is it me, or is she suddenly incredibly gorgeous?" His eyes gazed after her longingly.

"Let her go, Snow. Let her go."

Chapter 12
Heartbroken

"Look, dude, there's no way this is going to work," I growled as I flattened my body up against the padded wall of the Pordunce Elementary gymnasium.

"Not with that attitude, it won't. Hashbrown, you need to concentrate."

Bad attitude or no, Camo Phillips was out of his mind if he believed I could be camouflaged standing next to a bright red gymnastics' pad while wearing a powder blue sweat suit.

"Why do I have to wear this outfit again?" I asked, staring down at my ridiculous attire.

Camo frowned. "It's all part of the training, Hashbrown. Besides, it's the only one I could get on such short notice, so don't stretch it out. My sister will have a fit if she finds out I'm using it."

"Your sister?" I asked, looking down at my clothes in shock. "These are your sister's clothes?"

I had never worn girl's clothes before. This was a first for me. Let me correct that. It was almost a first. There was that time a year ago when Snow Cone and I had to go incognito to unravel the mystery behind the Girl Scout's exploding Thin Mints. That was at least a worthy cause.

"I think I'm going to call it a day," I said, removing the frilly jacket and noticing for the first time the floral pattern sewn on the inside. It was reversible for crying out loud.

"But you're making excellent progress."

"I don't think holding my breath for twenty seconds with my head dunked in cooling chicken grease and trying to disappear against a gymnastics pad wearing your sister's sweat suit is what I'd call progress." This was ridiculous. I started to seriously regret my enrollment in this after school, self-defense class. It was Snow Cone's idea, but we were probably being a little too cautious. Things had settled down for a while after the Hambone incident. It's safe to say most of the everyday activities returned to normal. Normal, that is, for Pordunce Elementary.

The Figanewty Organization had crumbled with the loss of Cordovo and Tony Ten Fingers. There were a few odd crimes committed now and then, a tack stuck in a teacher's chair or a tuna taped to the bottom of the drinking fountain, but that was to be expected. Someone had to break up the monotony.

Hambone went inactive from the public bully sector, but he was by no means a normal student—let's be honest, the kid shaved already and had biceps on top of biceps. But the bullying stopped almost completely. In fact, there were a few incidents where he actually spoke to me in the hallways.

Hambone and Luinda were very much in love. He attended all of her wrestling matches, which improved her record significantly. Seriously, who would dare beat her in a match now she that had Hambone as her boyfriend?

The two of them were always being shooed out of the hallways to get to class. It was disgusting and should have been illegal, but as long as it kept Hambone off the warpath, it was worth it to have to endure their sappy jabbering.

Measles's doctor diagnosed him with malaria and mumps but eventually reversed the diagnoses. Yep. You guessed it, measles again. There was a silver lining to that cloud, however. The local university hand-selected Measles from a long list of sickly students to test out a new prescription pill. They haven't figured out how to cure his measles yet, but the pill has made his skin soft and supple. Plus, he says he can see through walls, but we're not completely convinced of that.

Bubblegum Bulkins continues to do what he does best— chew gum and lots of it. He secretly started a collection of his most favorite flavors of bubble gum and kept a stash of it under his desk during English class. That was all fine and dandy up until the day Mr. Coppercork noticed the colorful array of rubbery stalactites dangling from Bubblegum's desktop. As punishment, Bubblegum got a week's worth of detention scraping the gum off of all the tables throughout the entire school. He absolutely loved it, and now volunteers to perform the service on a daily basis for free. No one has figured out what he does with all the gum, but the trashcans are always empty when he leaves for the day.

Four Hips went on a diet until he found out what a diet really was.

"No way am I cutting down on my eating. That's not healthy!" he had shouted at the family dietician. They managed to cut his eating down to one trumpet case full of food a day, but there is no telling how long that will last. Four Hips swears he is wasting away to nothing.

Whiz was a celebrity for a while. His story about surviving a day in the water tank could be heard around every corner of the school. Although he constantly stretched the truth of what really happened on that dreary afternoon, the rest of the students still loved every bit of it. The latest version of his tale involves him trying to stay afloat during a mini-hurricane that erupted in the tank and narrowly avoiding a school of starving piranhas while battling the watery ghost of a cyclops named Igor. It's a really good one, and he says he intends to write it down.

Snow Cone was heartbroken over Luinda for about a month, which I'll never understand. Something about how he found her heroics on the playground to be a sign of true beauty.

Barf! Give me a break.

At least he finally got over her and now has his eyes set on Brandy Newspickle. Fat chance of that ever happening. I promised to support my best friend in all of his choices no matter how ridiculous they are. Along with all of Snow Cone's many duties in the club, he has actually taken over the responsibility of finding new recruits. Next week's enlistment will include Pigeon Criggle and the student formally known as "The Sheik." We're going to need a bigger tree house.

Misty Piccolo was my girlfriend for about a week. It was glorious . . . well, somewhat glorious. She was so impressed at how I stood up to Hambone, despite being on the verge of death, that she couldn't help but fall in love. Who could blame her? My popularity at Pordunce skyrocketed after the showdown.

Life was good until the day my science project was due. I had completely forgotten about it. After trying to fib my way through my part of the presentation, I got tongue tied and opted to belch the alphabet while hopping on one foot.

Ms. Pinkens wasn't impressed. She gave us a C- for our grade, and I received a nice two-page note from Misty after class telling me she was breaking up with me. She rambled on and on about how she needed a more sensitive boyfriend.

Sensitive? Hello, I'm eleven-years old. The most sensitive

I can give you is how I tear up when I help my mom whip up onion soup.

I suppose I was a little upset after the breakup, but considering the fact it was Misty Piccolo, I actually bounced back quicker than expected.

The weeks are flying by rapidly and soon school will let out for Christmas vacation. I must say I'm hoping to see a laser-guided crossbow with my name on it tucked neatly beneath our tree. Yeah, I suppose it's a wish only a hash brown could ask for, and I'm sure there will be a few concerned parents when they see me toting that beautiful weapon up into my tree house. But do you think I'll hear any complaints after I successfully eliminate the neighborhood woodpecker problem? No sir.

To be honest, I'm going to miss school. I love learning. Okay, that's not honest. I'm going to miss my friends that live out of my neighborhood. Of course, I'll see Snow Cone Jones every single day, along with Four Hips, Measles, Bubblegum, and Whiz. But there are new faces in my circle of friends that desperately need my attention.

I'm going to miss the regular routine of life at Pordunce Elementary for the two weeks while we're gone. No rabid squirrels chucking acorns to avoid, or tiny albino first graders zooming through the halls like humming birds hopped up on sugar for that matter.

Truthfully, it really is a great school. I don't care what people say about it being an unsafe educational institution. That's complete garbage. Who cares if the grounds used to be a nuclear testing site? Most of the kids actually enjoy the fact that they glow in the dark when the lights are out. It solves the problem of not having a night light.

Plus, you'll never hear me complain about how Pordunce Elementary was selected as a pilot school that allowed convicted criminals to student teach. Learning how to carve a weapon out of soap and to break prison bars with tightly wound toilet paper is what I call an education.

Pordunce Elementary is my stomping ground, and I doubt I'd be happier in any other school. It's the best place for my friends and a hotspot for adventure. I can't wait for the next one.

Wsidom of the Oracle: A top-secret guide to the Riff Raff at Pordunce

So I suppose you want to know what only the Great Oracle knows, do you? I guess I can't blame you. It is truly amazing what my eyes see, but this information doesn't come cheap, if you know what I mean. I expect payment. One can never have too many Rip Strapinski baseball cards. . . .

Hashbrown Winters (Flinton Deanderbow Winters), 5th grade: I still remember the day when he out ate Butter Bibowski in that ridiculous hash brown eating contest. So he has a tree house . . . so what? I had a tree house once; now I have a locker, but no one's invited to see inside it.

Snow Cone Jones (Pierre Yosepa Jones), 5th grade: Dared by Pinata Gonzales to eat a parking cone filled with dirty, lemon-flavored snow. Only I'm pretty sure it wasn't lemon.

Whiz Peterson (Charlie Mac Peterson), 5th grade: Latest birthday gifts include rubber pants, rubber sheets, and a moving sidewalk that runs from his bed all the way to the toilet.

Four Hips Dixon (Leslie Kip Dixon), 5th grade: Banned from every all-you-can eat buffet in the county. No one's safe when his hunger rages, not even polar bears.

Measles Mumphrey (Zachery Lewis Mumphrey), 5th grade: That boy has an itching problem, and one of his measles looks exactly like Queen Cleopatra.

Bubblegum Bulkins (Eric Isaac Bulkins), 5th grade: Has gone his entire grade school career chewing bubble gum every day, even during lunch. Don't bother asking me how he managed doing that on the day they served creamed asparagus soufflé.

Hambone Oxcart, 5th grade: Apparently he is really mean and eats wood. People call him the number one bully at Pordunce Elementary, but he's never really bothered me. Of course, he generally tries to avoid talking lockers.

Misty Piccolo, 5th grade: Beauty, perfect grades, perfect teeth, and she's every teacher's pet . . . I see no real value.

Tony Ten Fingers (Tony Namoth Spelunker), 6th grade: The muscle behind the Figanewty Organization. Has locked countless students into their lockers, and yet they've all somehow made it home for dinner. Where's the justice in that?

Cordovo Figanewty, 6th grade—supposedly: I laughed so hard I cried the day the Figanewty family pushed the teaching staff out of the lounge and into the janitorial closet. Ha! See how you like tight, enclosed spaces! I will say this though, with all of Cordovo's moving around to different schools over the years, I'm pretty sure he should be graduated from high school by now. But what do I know? I'm only the Oracle!

Luinda "The Manatee" Sharpie, 4th grade: I don't typically shower praises down upon the heads of my classmates, especially anyone that goes by the name of Manatee, but Luinda has a gift. I know it may be difficult to believe, but you didn't see her cartwheel kick that boy who made fun of her braces.

Teeter-Totter Williams (Allen Roger Williams), 6th grade: Really, what are parents feeding kids these days? My advice would be to avoid the teeter totters, the see-saws, and pretty much any playground device that could be used as a launching pad when this kid is around.

Pigeon Criggle (Donald Cal Criggle), 1st grade: What a pest! Fluttering and squealing this way and that. Somebody needs to put that boy in a cage or stuff a cracker in his mouth for the love of Pete!

Paul "The Shiek" Rumspill, 6th grade: Plays a mean flute, but no one's supposed to know about that. He also wore a turban to school for three years just because he could.

Razor Cannelloni (Louis Cannelloni), 6th grade: Another trouble maker. Tends to sharpen anything he can get his hands on. Pencils, erasers, chocolate bars, students. . . .

Squid Madsen (Marcus Madsen), 6th grade: He's somewhat of a master at giving swirlies. I hear they can be quite refreshing.

Tommy Pastrami (Tommy Rudebager), 6th grade: Infamous first half of the sandwich twins. Eats nothing but sandwiches.

Petey Provolone (Pete Lumbunts), 6th grade: Infamous second half of the sandwich twins. Eats nothing but sandwiches.

Butter Bibowski (Lintel Montgomery Bibowski), 5th grade: An artist of sorts, he once made an exact replica of the Statue of Liberty out of nothing but mounds of unsalted butter.

Pot Roast Oberham (Gregory Oberham), 5th grade: Brings his lunch in a crock-pot and frequently wows the students with his fabulous recipes. You should try his crêpes. They are wonderful and fit perfectly through a locker slot.

Stilts Drubbers (Ethan Oakley), 5th grade: As far as doctors can tell, his body is missing his torso. His legs actually start right beneath his armpits.

Piñata Gonzales (Calvin Fred Gonzales), 5th grade: Is always sneaking into school with gobs of wrapped candies in his pockets. I can usually tell where he's been just by watching the swarms of first graders eating his dropped gumdrops off the floor.

Staples Ardmore (Larry Mort Ardmore), 5th grade: What a klutz. He no longer has feeling in any of his fingers, his elbows or his belly button. Some dares just aren't worth going through with.

Petrol Giminski (Harold Giminski) 5th grade: His family runs one of the local gas stations. He smells of unleaded fuel and once took a bath in motor oil.

Camo Phillips (Roderick Bismuth Phillips), 5th grade: I'm not too fond of this sneaky one. It's embarrassing really, but I once carried on a conversation with him for fifteen minutes, thinking I was chatting with the drinking fountain.

Radar Munski (Matthew Joseph Munski), 5th grade: Rumor has it he can hear the late bell ringing before the principal actually pushes it.

Saddle Bags Bollinger (Shad Olaf Bollinger), 5th grade: Whatever you do, don't go horseback riding with him. Not a pretty sight . . . so I've heard.

The Oracle (Gabriel Yucatan), n/a: I rule this school! So what if I've been trapped in my locker for seven years? My information business is booming, and I have T-shirts on sale in the lunch room.

Discussion Questions

1. Almost all of the students at Pordunce Elementary have an unusual nickname. If you attended that school, what would be your nickname and what would be the story behind it?
2. Hashbrown Winters has many friends and a really cool club. What do you think it is about Hashbrown that makes him liked by almost everyone?
3. When Hashbrown goes out to meet Hambone on the playground, he is surprised to see all of his closest friends walking out with him despite the danger. What does that tell you about his friends?
4. What was your favorite part of the story? The funniest scene? Your favorite character?
5. If your school had an "all-seeing Oracle" living in the lockers, and you were allowed to ask him one free question, what would it be?
6. What items would be included in your survival kit?
7. Have you ever had trouble with a bully? How did you get out of it? Do you think Hashbrown's tactics would have worked in your situation?

About the Author

Frank L. Cole was born in a quiet town in Kentucky where he spent most of his childhood sharing exaggerated stories for show and tell. He now lives in Utah with his wife and three children.

One of Frank's greatest claims to fame was when he was rushed to the emergency room as a third-grader after falling out of Hashbrown Winter's tree house. If he had a nickname it would be Frankie the Phantom.

The Adventures of Hashbrown Winters is Frank's debut novel. You can find out more about Frank L. Cole and Hashbrown Winters by visiting www.hashbrownwinters.com.

0 26575 53030 8